BRYAN JACKSON

THE GAME
DON'T WAIT
1, 2, 3

Paperback ISBN: 978-1-63616-080-1

Published By Opportune Independent Publishing Co.
www.opportunepublishing.com

Printed in the United States of America
For permission requests, email the author with the subject line as "Attention: Permissions Coordinator" to the email address below:

Info@opportunepublishing.com

GAME DON'T WAIT

Ms. M was still devastated after the loss of Big Girl. Also devastated were her son, Marty, and her daughter, who never really got to know her mother, let alone the circumstances behind her mother's death. Luscious Bell had been delirious, as well; she was quite distraught for months.

Her daughter's funeral had been one of the largest in Casa Grande, Arizona. So many people had looked up to and admired Big Girl, the "Goddess of Basketball." In the eyes of so many, she was their friend.

Friendships these days are so few and far between. There is no loyalty or honor, let alone peace, because of this dog-eat-dog environment that has become a plague of the worst kind. It is even sad to say the motto, "Trust no one," let alone bitches of every kind. During the loss of Big Girl, many of her friends came by to check on her children, and 99 percent came by to be nosy.

Seeing that Luscious Bell had begun to lose her footing, the devil was able to do what he does best…. steal, kill and destroy. Coming in various ways, shapes and forms, Satan will come through our friends. If he cannot be like a mountain bell, reaching out to touch somebody, he will not think twice about coming through the very ones we love the most. This makes their betrayal even more unbelievable because we thought they loved us, only to find it was all a figment of our wildest imagination. How does that song go? "It takes a fool to learn that love don't love nobody…" God's love is a solid foundation that brings you salvation, endowing your very being with trust and filling your cup with faith that can move mountains. Reading the parable in which Jesus was labeled the "Friend of Sinners," we see that this is the friend we all need in our lives. He did not care about all the victories or the prideful things that we as a people love to do today. You did not find Jesus amongst the rich and prideful, but in the presence of those who were poor in mind, body, spirit or soul. Our friend wanted better for others than he wanted for himself.

In every relationship of every kind, there must be sacrifice—sometimes done by me, sometimes done by you—for God loves a cheerful giver. As it is said, it is better to give than receive, yet you will not see too many friends doing too much of that, let alone family members. Therefore, my friend today is Jesus, because he said he would never leave me or forsake me. How many friends promised to have your back while you did something for them, yet, like it says in the Bible, played possum, seeking out the windows and wanting you to come back when the sun was up? Then, it was too late… Thank you, but no, thank you! Like predator to prey, or a buzzard or vulture, the so-called friends of Big Girl began to darken her mother's doorstep, bringing in legions of unseen dark spirits and seeking to dwell, each having an ulterior motive.

Luscious Bell was weak; in her weakness, actors were able to slip through the cracks. Therefore, we must stay focused on the prize, not looking to the left or the right. Heaven forbids you to look back, proclaiming that if you do so, you are no longer fit for the kingdom of Heaven. You see, sin had already made its way into Luscious Bell's home through the second husband, Mr. Sea. Mr. Sea was married to another woman while entertaining thoughts of being slick. The same thing that makes you laugh will make you cry. After Big Girl's passing, Luscious Bell did what she knew how to do: She looked out for the best interest of the children and quit work. This led her to depend on her husband, which made him turn away from her, his good wife, the mother of his children. Sin became the same wedge that brought separation in his first marriage. Alcohol became the focus of Mr. Sea's life. In the battle of alcohol versus Luscious Bell, alcohol became the victor.

Therefore, Mr. Sea separated from his home, heading out the door and away from another good woman. He thought that just because she may have needed him, it was all right to step on her a few times. *She ain't gon' complain, he thought.* He was wrong!

She had too much respect for herself, as well as morals and values that she lived by. Above all, she had a friend in Jesus, who brought her through storms of fire before. She knew that if he did it before, he would do it again.

Standing on his promises in truth, trust and faith, she was able to walk away. Knowing that God had promised to never leave her or forsake her, she was able to find more strength and power than she ever dreamed of. The balance between seeking a blessing and expecting a blessing is everything. If your balance is off, a whole lot of other things will be off, too. Our equilibrium must be stable in order for us to make sound, stable decisions; we must be grounded and anchored on a solid foundation to be saved. Without Mr. Sea or a job, money had to be budgeted because of Luscious's fixed income. The plumbing in the bathroom and kitchen had busted, ruining the carpet throughout the house. So, there wouldn't be funds coming from the insurance company until they did what they had to do. Luscious Bell remembered the guy who did all the work for Big Girl because he was one of those friends who called to check on Mama Bell. Calling him opened a whole new can of worms and problems.

"Hey, Ted. How are you doing?" Luscious Bell asked.

"Not too, good Mrs. Lemons. I'm moving out of my house, and I got no place to stay. My wife is divorcing me."

"I'm sorry to hear that, Ted." Not wanting to add her burdens to his cross, she allowed a minute of silence to pass between them.

"What can I do for you, though?" he asked.

"I don't want to bother you with my problems. Don't worry about it," Luscious said.

"Now… now, Mrs. Lemons, I was just caught up in the moment. My bad. How can I help you?" Ted inquired.

"Ted, I am having plumbing problems, and water is all over the house. I need it taken care of as soon as possible."

"I've got nothing better to do," Ted replied. "How do I get to Casa Grande?"

"Right off I-10 West on the Tucson exit."

"I'll be there in a couple of hours and will get all your maintenance taken care of." Ted said.

That is how he ended up living with Luscious Bell. Her kindness—the God and Holy Spirit that dwelled in her—would never allow her to turn anyone down.

Even though Tommy Jr., Lil Mama and TJ were her children, Luscious Bell was a very independent woman who took care of her own as she taught her children. With that said, everyone had their own lives, and she did not start to enjoy her own. With that out of the way, she needed to call Sanders & Sanders to begin a divorce with Mr. Sea. So, she dialed the number that she had on speed dial. She had become good friends with his wife, Gladys, who was out saving the world in her oncology field.

"Sanders & Sanders Law Offices," the receptionist said.

"Yes, this is Luscious Bell Lemons. May I please speak to Arthur?"

"His line is busy; would you like to hold? I will put you through as soon as he's off the line."

"Yes, sure. I'll hold."

The receptionist put on some gospel music as they played "How Great Thou Art." Luscious Bell murmured to the peaceful music until the line was answered.

"This is Arthur. To whom do I owe the honor? How are you?""Above all, I am blessed, but I need you to settle my divorce with Mr. Sea because we can't seem to remain headed in the right direction," Luscious replied.

"I have no problems, let alone questions, because your mind seems to be made up. Shall we say, irreconcilable circumstances?" Arthur asked.

"Surely, that would be fine," she said.

"I will be in the area in three weeks, for your son,

TJ's, Naughty's and Sheriff's weddings. Tracy and my wife are looking forward to it. We'll be having Lady and Sweet accompanying us to the festival of the three couples getting married," Arthur said.

"Well, will we be able to square it all away then?"

Arthur laughed. "Sounds like you're pushing him out the door!"

"One thing about being an adult in the prime of your maturity: You go through what you want to go through. These children like to go around once or twice to see what works. I am an old-fashioned gal who had hopes of making it right, but he done headed on back to his first wife, which is best for us all," Luscious Bell said.

"You're right, family. I'll see you at the wedding, then," Arthur said.

"Give Gladys my love and respect, and I'll see you good people then, God willing.

"Yes, God willing." Arthur hung up.

Truth is, the whole wedding thing had somehow slipped Luscious's mind, and she felt bad because her son, TJ, deserved the best. TJ had not only been getting ready to get married, but had graduated and was in his second year of school to become a radiologist. So, yes, she really had to step up as a mother. She dialed the number.

"Hello there, Mother. I love you and I was just thinking

of you how wonderful you always are. Thank you," TJ said.

"Great minds do think alike, and I was sitting here thinking of all you've achieved in your life. I am immensely proud of you, son, and your daddy would've been so proud of you! Son, you are a spitting image of that man, through and through! Like, I ain't participated one bit bringing you into this world."

"Hold on, Luscious Bell Grande," TJ said jokingly to his mother. "But you did! If I did not have anything else, I would have your heart. That is more of a blessing than I could count in my life, as well as those of mine who will follow."

Luscious Bell was quite taken aback as she heard her son say that. It was not the fact that he said that because he always has said kind things; it was *when* he said it that made it even sweeter.

"Thank you, son! I wanted to host a dinner for you and Teka on your graduation night. Teka will be here then, and my daughter-in-law and I haven't really gotten to talk since Big Girl's passing. So, we will be able to chop it up a bit. Also, I would like you both to have my wedding ring and your father's, even though you already have your own. I know that you will do more than cherish them, but wear them, too. That would bring your mama so much joy, and surely make your father proud, 'cause you're just like him!

"Thanks a lot, Mom! You made my day!"

"No, baby—you always make mine. Thank you," Luscious replied.

"Oh! The lady called about the dress, so I just paid for it. I'll pick it up when I go to pick up the boxes from Lil Mama and Tyrik," TJ said.

"How they been doing?"

"What you mean, Ma? You haven't talked to your daughter this week? Or are you still feeling some type of way about your grandbabies?"

"The devil is a liar!" she laughed. "TJ, let me go, 'cause I'm going to hurt you when I see you for passing licks like that to your mama! I love you, baby."

"Love you, too. And call my sister!"

Luscious laughed and hung up. She then dialed Lil Mama, then said to herself, *Let me go ahead and do a roll call to make sure my children are all right.* The phone rang three times, and Lil Mama picked up.

"Big Girl! Sweet, sexy and sassy," Lil Mama answered.

"My daughter sure is! How's Mama's baby?" Luscious Bell asked.

"I'm doing good, Ma. I'm just here, paying bills and waiting for the girls to come home from school. We all been doing good. How are you?" Lil Mama replied.

"Good! Just got off the phone with your brother, TJ. I

gave him my rings and your dad's, since he's the baby. That's good. Did he tell you about your dress? He said that when he picks up your deliveries, he's going to pick it up. How's Tyrik doing, and his grandma?"

"They coo'… Tyrik's driving me crazy about wanting to get married and have another baby, but I told him, 'I don't hear no biological clock of mine ticking no time soon.' Plus, I want to finish college and pursue my life's dream of becoming an author to reach out and help others."

"You could do both, baby, if you want to. You have come an exceptionally long way, and I am so proud of you. Keep up the good work. Follow your dream, and never sacrifice your happiness for anyone or anything," Luscious Bell said.

"Mama, I got a crowd coming in, so let me go. I love you!" Lil Mama said.

"I love you, too!" Luscious Bell said.

She dialed Tommy Jr.'s phone.

"Hello! Hold on, whoever this is!" he cursed at others in the room. "Hello? I'm sorry," he said.

"You better be, 'cause I was fixin; to come and scalp you. Wash ya mouth out with soap!"

"My bad, Ma. These kids just getting on my last nerve!"

"Welcome to being a parent! Hello!"

"Here we go! I love my kids, but they ain't gon' run this electric bill up! I don't care how much the NBA wants to pay me!"

"Well, don't you be too rough on my grandkids, or else I'ma skin you alive!"

"I won't, Ma! We ready for the wedding of the century! It's gon' be nice," TJ said.

"Yes, son, it is! How's Marty doing up there? Is he better?"

"He is. His godfather, M&M, stays on him, so he is absolutely doing better than he was."

After the circumstances of his mother's death, as any child would, Marty got out of control to the point that Luscious Bell felt he needed a male role model in his life. So she sent him to live with his uncle, TJ. Marty was the presence of his godfather, M&M, who gave him the crucial man-to-man moments, always allowing Marty to ask any questions and also giving him the permission to call him at any given moment. Marty was now going on 15 years old and still doing good in school. Since he was doing good in school, M&M asked Luscious Bell if he could buy him a car.

After school, Marty worked at his mother's Boys and Girls Club, which would soon be his. Sweet, Sassy and Sexy would be his sister's someday. She was turning three years old. She spent most of her time with her father figure, who loved her; Luscious Bell didn't have a problem with him being a father to his child. He knew that his daughter would need him for the rest of her life. Stepping up to the plate, he didn't want to leave any chance of her being misled. Therefore, in all he did, he made sure that things that were done in front of his daughter were positive, as well as beneficial to her well-being. Sheriff, TJ and Naughty had been at the store when TJ was on the phone with his mother, and they were calling him a Mama's boy. "That's right—I cannot get mad at the truth," he laughed.

Opening the cell phone store and barbershop had become even more lucrative to the delivery service. Since Shardom was no longer in business next door, the owner of that space wanted to get rid of it after he became ill with cancer. So, he presented the building to these young fellas at a low cost, since they had been doing a lot for the community in working with Casa Grande Cares Counseling. Arthur at Sanders & Sanders law offices had been taking care of the business aspect of Team Naughty Boys, Inc.

"So, fellas, graduation will be here soon. Do we have our homes in order to bring our new in-laws into each of our homes?" Sheriff asked.

"I am! I'm ready to get my grown man on and do what's good for a young brother!" Naughty said. After his close call with doing life for supposedly taking Mitch's life, he no longer took life for granted, let alone his freedom. He didn't want to end up on a cold slab like Man-Man.

"I'm ready, too! Since Uncle Arthur is coming down for the wedding, are we going to let him take care of the closing of the sale of the building?"

"Yeah, he was going to get the legal ball rolling," Naughty said.

"Good! Don't forget, Tracy's coming down, too, and we can make a nice donation to Days Transitional Housing for God's People," Sheriff said.

"Is that guilt money because you used to grill our cousin and headbutt her when we used to play marbles outside of Nanny Sister's house?" TJ asked.

"He used to try to play the good one to spin her to get her money," Naughty laughed.

"It was your idea, Naughty!" Sheriff shot back. "Now, the ugly duckling done turned into not just a swan, but also your cousin! Now, who's ugly?!" They all started laughing as the store phone began to ring.

"Naughty Boys, Inc. ... Hey, Abdul! How you and Lety doing? Y'all have your baby yet?" TJ said as he turned on the speaker phone function.

"We sure did! A boy! Abdul Jones Gutierrez."

"Congratulations! How's Lety?"

"She good! She right here!"

"Hi, guys. I'm all right," she said shyly.

"Congratulations!" They all said again.

"Thank you! Seems like the baby didn't want to miss the wedding!" Lety said. "Guess not! Thanks, Lil Ab, because I would have been lost!" Naughty said.

"Me, too!" Sheriff and TJ agreed.

"Well, fellas, let me go so I can spread the news and start getting ready for the trip!"

"See you then! We can't wait to see y'all again," Naughty said.

"It's been a minute, huh?" Abdul asked.

"It has, but it's cool because I didn't want to have to tumble like we used to," Naughty said.

"You mean when I slapped that wig back!"

"Right! Wait till you get here!" Sheriff said.

"Love you, too, cuzzo!" Ab said.

Feeling overjoyed and filled with love, Ab called his cousin, Tracy Sanders, Uncle Arthur's daughter.

"Days Transitional Housing for God's People! Lady speaking."

"Hey, Lady! How y'all doing? And the babies?"

"Good! James is going crazy, but we good," Lady said.

"We're just calling to let you know we had the baby and

to make sure y'all still coming to the wedding—because we will be there, after all!" Ab said.

"Yes, Tracy, Sweet and I will be riding with Uncle Arthur," she said.

"That's cool! Just wanted y'all to know," Ab said.

"I'm here by myself, unless you would like to invite a few of Ivy's occupants," Lady said jokingly.

"Yeah, bring them! The more, the merrier! I'll pass on the info. See you then, and congrats to you all!" Lady replied.

"Thanks, cuzzo!" Ab said.

It was a blessing to see and hear of a family's good news instead of always bad news, of deaths or funerals. Ab felt blessed to have a prosperous family that shared each other's burdens, as well as their accomplishments, to sharpen the iron and inspire those who had lost their way or lost hope. Good rays of sunshine and becomes a beacon that can eliminate the possible darkness in different areas of one's life. Communication is a form of love to say a person's loved ones matter, as it builds the trust and confidence needed in life.

Aunt Sharon and Teka had barely come in from getting her dress refitted for what seemed like the thousandth time…

"Just to be sure," Teka said. She was so worried about gaining a few pounds that would be seen before her beauty. Teka, Daisha and Dulce were all going to drive to Casa Grande with Aunt Sharon so they all could get ready for the wedding together and be there for the graduations of their family members and better halves. Each one of these girls had their dresses made of French silk with pearl sequins in all the right places, complementing each part to give hints of love, suspense and passion to their future husbands. Being all French silk, the most expensive and almost extinct in America to obtain, all three dresses were designed with love created from the most important night of these young girls' lives.

Each had vowed to remain a virgin until they married so they would have the special gift of their virginity to give their spouses. They, too, had vowed to each create a gown of all their hopes and dreams to tauntingly tease the love of their lives… their soulmates. Each girl would be leaving their homes for good, taking all the different things that had each made for each other these last few months.

The girls would all be staying at Aunt Sha's house, with them and Sharon moving to their homes that they had thought they would have to find. But due to their thoroughness and caliber, the grooms-to-be had already been on top getting homes to give to their wives as gifts to cherish for a lifetime. Aunt Sha and Aunt Sharon always had a sisterly relationship before Paco the pervert stepped into the picture. These two became Ms. Charlesetta's gambling buddies who hooked up with Aunt Mary and Aunt Exa Viola. There was nothing this crew wouldn't do for each other in life, even when going to casinos or bingo halls. They had been periodically getting together at different times; whether one was on the east coast or the west coast, they made it happen. They brought happiness together as they cooked and hustled together every time. Marty had been getting ready to catch the bus home and was already plotting on the dude from Central who had beef with him when someone in a new gray Jaguar with limo-tinted windows pulled up and blew the horn. He couldn't see anything but white teeth smiling back at him. Marty said to himself, *Who is dis pussy who keep pressing up on me in this car, then blowing the horn?!* Right when Marty was about to get on the person's level, M&M rolled down the window.

"What up, young buck?" I see you was ready to get lifted in dis peace! On me!" M&M said, laughing.

"It ain't even that type of time, Godfather, but wait! You got a new whip?! When you gon' let ya boy sport this thing?" Marty asked.

"Whenever you get your driver's license, you'll be good to go, son. This is you!" M&M said.

"What are you spinning me for, Paps?" Marty asked.

"Now, real people do real things! You've been doing good in school and at work, and with the other children. Son, you are doing so much better now. For a minute after Moms passed, you was like a loose cannon. You had us all worried, 'cause more than anything, we love you and want you to survive. Your mother always wanted the absolute best for you for years. After your sister was born, she wanted it even more for you both. Your mother was like a daughter to me for many years, and I always wanted the best for her. I would talk to her just like I am talking to you. Your mother had a will of her own, and she wouldn't let anyone in her square when it came to you, not even your dad. So, with you getting it in like you've been in a major way. I want you to know your mom still loves you. We are here to let you know we care. We are paying attention and appreciate the positive aspects of your life."

Marty was crying now after hearing all the things his mother had kept bottled up. This is what he needed to hear from someone he looked up to. Moments before M&M drove up, he had already been planning to go upside the boy from Central's head. First, though, he was gon' holla at a blood nigga who would have his back on any day, but he had to join their crew and get jumped in first. Until Godfather pulled up on him, he was headed in all the wrong directions. In life, it's always easy to cast our cares to the wind when we feel like no one cares or even pays attention. When we voice our love, as well as alertness in our actions, this shows your love for others, rather than just talking about it.

When you exchange things with others, or words as simple as "I love you," as well as showing each other your love, too, you can save each other's lives. Who knows what the next man thinks, let alone what he's going through?

When a child or a person is constantly getting yelled at, communication becomes few and far between because this person wishes to sever the lines they still have with their abuser. They aren't trying to hear it. That is when things will get worse for all concerned parties. This child or person then no longer has a sounding board, as the molehills have become mountains of stumbling blocks that will soon be volcanoes ready to erupt. When the eruption happens, who knows which direction the hot lava will go in? This will ruin not only their lives, but everyone's, as one spoiled apple ruins the bunch.

So, when M&M stepped up to the plate with love and praise to Marty for doing the right things, it made Marty want to do even better for himself 'cause he realized people cared about him. A lot of times, just hearing or even feeling expressions of love becomes a ripple effect within someone's life. As there are seasons, there are times to plant and time to nourish, just as there are surely times of discipline. These times of discipline let Marty know the rules of the day. He knew that he got the car because of his obedience, and he would be able to keep it by maintaining this obedience.

M&M had parked at Tommy Jr.'s house, where Marty was staying. So, when he left, he would leave the car, giving it to Marty to keep and therefore do as he was advised: wait till he got his permit and furthermore. The car being there was an incentive, as well as motivation for Marty to remain responsible, trustworthy and obedient as a child who wanted good things in life.

Tyrik was a bit nervous to see Naughty and Sheriff because he hadn't seen them; they had beef since things went down with Raheem and Man Man. .

He had seen TJ on numerous occasions because he was with TJ's sister. He also kept TJ up to date on Big Girl's son, Marty, making sure he pulled his weight at the gym because it would be his one day. Truth is, everyone was praying and hoping Marty would find his way into the NBA. But, of course, they wanted it to be his decision, so they didn't want him to feel like he was being pressured into fulfilling his mother's dream, but his own. Coming from prison, having to have to start over in a new place was interesting for Tyrik, and it remained so.

His grandmother, Charlesetta, told him what he was involved in on the streets of Philly was also here in Arizona. So, he had to make a choice to change. He would always be himself, and more than anything, you can't run from yourself. If the hustle game is still in you, you must use ingenuity to transcend the positive into the equation. Then, you must remove all the negativities to find a solidified balance that would keep you anchored in your life, never taking your freedom for granted in any way.

Tyrik learned that the dudes on the block didn't give any flying chucks about him. All they cared about was how easy he made it for them each time he sacrificed his livelihood to fatten frogs for snakes. When he got sent to the bucket, all their hood and the block did was talk bad about a nigga and laugh at him, saying how stupid he was. It's always been said that when you know better, you do better, which is true. Then, you are able to ground yourself in love, peace, joy and happiness for yourself, thus giving you the ability to plant the same seeds into other's lives, as you have set an example.

Tyrik learned from his mistakes and did not repeat them, but moved forward to do things for and with his family who loved and supported him when the block or his so-called friends turned their backs on him. With friends or homies like that, you don't even need enemies! For us, as people, to learn different things in our lives that we deem to be good for our lives at one time or another, we are drawn to these people to learn these very lessons in order to survive in the world that we live in today. Picking friends is like picking a significant other. My sister always told me, "You are no better than the friends you keep," which is true.

Their ways become yours, and vice versa! So, pray for discernment in picking your friends. Make your own decisions and stand by them. While playing the game OneMan, Tyrik learned that people step on one another to get to the top— that's why it's called a game. It's all a figment of your imagination because what goes up must come down! While Tyrik was doing his bid in the Feds, he had time to think over the things he did in his life. With his bid being all said and done, he was able to analyze all aspects of his life under his life's microscope and dissect the good, as well as the bad, decisions in his life. This would help him find the balance and foundation needed to place himself on solid grounds so when stories of any kind came, he could stand firm until the waters were under the bridge.

He found that nothing was worth sacrificing his freedom, nor the times he often took for granted, thinking that the world ended just for him. In retrospect, it goes on, because for real—for *real*—we had been in the way of a lot of our own goods, as well as our own evils. Tyrik also learned that the hustle game has been in the equation since time began, giving each who slayed the game the chance to step up to win or lose. Many have hopped on and won more than they should've, only to get greedy, then lose it all for shits and giggles. Then, niggas want to talk about what they used to have, but it means nothing to me or anybody else! Talk about what you have done for your kids—then, I'm impressed.

After you have lost to the game, and possibly have lost all the essential things and people who brought you true love or happiness, a gift horse often comes into your life and makes it whole through God's love and wisdom. The easiest way is never the best way. For example, getting something for free has no value, as opposed to you spending your chips on it. Only then would you do what needed to be done to take care of it and keep it. Tyrik had thought about all of this as he set aside the legacy Big Girl built up for him as she lived off the fruits of other people's harvests. When Big Girl died, Tyrik came across Big Girl's stash of cash—close to a million dollars. He figured he deserved it since he found it. After sitting on it for a couple years, he got thirsty for the game that his two partners had already lost. Tyrik thought about all he would be sacrificing. He thought about the time he spent feeling betrayed and wanting to get even with others, only to realize he had no one else to blame but himself, for he chose the path of destruction for his life after his grandmother had worked so hard for him to have a better life.

After looking back over his life, he knew that in order to go any further in life, he had to forgive all the people he wanted or thought he needed to get even with—not for anyone else, but for himself. From that moment on, he knew that the game changed, so he embraced positivity and anchored himself into a life worth living. Beginning with the money he found, he knew he had to sow seeds of truth, love and honesty with Lil Mama who had ridden harder for him than any soldier in the hood or on the block. He also knew that because of the God in Lil Mama, his grandmother was able to find peace after almost giving up when he lost the game, playing on the Feds' court. He thought about all of this as he was led to return the money to the family who needed it to secure the legacy that Big Girl had while she died trying to obtain better for herself in the wrong, easy way.

"What is this?!" Lil Mama asked. It was a beautifully colored Coach purse that had a lot of dust on it from being inside a file cabinet that was no longer used.

"It had to be Big Girl's," Tyrik said as Lil Mama began looking through it with her mouth wide open. She considered this blessing to be right on time because her mother had an excessively big mortgage on their house and thought no one knew she was struggling. She allowed Ted, who worked for Big Girl by remodeling her buildup, to move in with her after he fixed the plumbing and put new carpet inside of her house. Her mother's pride didn't allow her to lean on her children.

Luscious Bell had let Satan in to steal, kill and destroy, to the point of losing her very mind, along with a lot of earthly treasures she had to pass on to her children. Yet, because she was anchored in the Lord, He did not leave her or forsake her, but brought a very much-needed light to shine upon her darkness before it got even worse. Lil Mama was observant, as she was taught through seeing her mother act like she didn't know, only to then rebuke Satan back to the very pits of hell where he needed to be with the help of God's love and divine intervention. It had been a few years back, when Big Girl had passed, that the devil was able to penetrate their lives— but not their souls. Being an on-time God, he led a friend of Lil Mama's, Del Rae, who worked at the bank that financed and reinforced a large mortgage for Luscious Bell without question. On this day, Del Rae had gotten in touch with Lil

Mama through TJ, telling him to get them in touch because she really needed her ASAP.

Since TJ had a childhood crush on this beautiful Del Rae, who looked as if she had fallen straight from heaven into the skating rink, he knew everything she had done for the sake of Lil Mama and remembered how she had been there in her time of need, even though they hadn't really kept in touch. Once she got there, they both started crying, vowing to keep in touch.

"Lil Mama, you're my friend, and what I tell you now could cause me to lose my job. But, for a good reason, I'm reaching out to you and risking something that could easily be replaced. Your mother's home will soon go into foreclosure. Something must be done, and I am willing to help," Del Rae said.

Right then and there, Lil Mama knew why she had been sitting on that money. She had slowly eased the large amount into the business account because she knew it belonged to Big Girl and suspected that Big Girl had been supplying Raheem, Man Man and Tyrik, although she hadn't known for sure. But it didn't matter because this money was right on time, considered a blessing that she would use to help her family get caught up on bills, because heaven forbid they end up as welfare recipients again. She did not think that she was too good to receive welfare, but she was not going to try to hustle the system after how blessed she now was. Although she knew that the great Charlesetta had the money to take them all out of the red and easily place them in the green, she was already paying rent for the house they stayed in. To keep up the businesses functioning, they had sold Big Girl's house. They gave her whip, which she had in her garage, to her daughter's father, and then sold the blazer, too.

"So, Del Rae, you really called to help me because you knew how I feel about you. I appreciate it, too! So, can you make a wire transfer from my account to pay off the mortgage?"

"Let's get on it, then!" Del Rae said.

Once that transaction cleared, she gave Lil Mama the receipts, clearance account and other materials, and no one was wiser to take on this task than Lil Mama. From there, Lil Mama headed on to her mother's house, saying nothing about the mortgage, but instead getting to the root of the problem. Ted pluck himself out the equation, receiving threats of prosecution if he returned or brought the funds up to Lil Mama's mother. She bought groceries and all the things needed for her mom's house and cleaned it up. Her mother had been in her bedroom in a drug-induced coma. After completing her mission, Lil Mama and Luscious Bell had a long talk that led to the whereabouts of Ted. Nothing was spoken about the house mortgage.

Spiritually, Luscious Bell was able to discern that her daughter knew what had been going on as she passed off the blame to Ted. She knew that her maker had been her intercessor and delivered the problem that she seemed unable to get rid of. In due season, as there are four, she knew that God had picked her up and placed her foot on solid ground again.

From that day to this one, she knew that God's grace and mercy were truly efficient, with the purpose of His glory achieved. As she prayed for her son, he, too, had been praying for her. He had heard through the grapevine about what had been going on, having occasionally even sat across the canal ditch on Friday and Saturday nights to pray. He knew she was a vessel of the Lord's. Prayer has always been powerful. If we prayed about others as much as we talked about them, can you imagine how many people would be healed as a whole? After failing in the eyes of the saints in church, at first, Luscious Bell had been embarrassed. That is, until the devil ran through her, and she spoke: "To hell with this!"

She headed to the church house, where she remains today. Luscious Bell found that her blessings came when she stood up and remained standing. From there, God picked her up and placed her back on solid ground, never leaving her or forsaking her, yet giving her the strength to weather the storms. As He brought her to them, He guided her through them.

The devil wants a lot of us to believe that after we have backslid in sin, we are not of any use thereafter. Know that is a lie from the very pit of hell. You get up, as He will give you strength to stand—and you will if you want to stand. Some people get comfortable at the bottom and don't want to get up. Getting up allows you to reap the harvest of what God has already promised you! Let it not be said that you were not able to get up, 'cause that, too, would be another lie from the devil. The spirit is willing, but the flesh is weak. We can do all things through Christ. As Lil Mama looked back upon her blessings, she knew only one could reach into each of their lives and bless them individually—that one would be God. Marty had just come from next door, where the gym was.

"Auntie, I'm going to take your trash out here, then go wash the towels and sheets on the office bed."

"That's fine. Thank you, Nephew!"

For a time, Marty wouldn't even bother to go into that room. At first, he blamed himself for his mother's death. His godfather, M&M, helped him to overcome his greatest fear of realizing that it wasn't his fault, but predestined before even she was born. One day, Marty had gone shopping. Everybody thought he was fixing up his room at his uncle Tommy house's, only to find that he had begun a new process of healing as he stepped back into that room, leaving Lil Mama scared and a little puzzled.

"Marty! You all right, Nephew?"

"Yes, Auntie. I'm just redecorating in here because

this bed hasn't had a comforter on it. My mama always said how she had loved this room that you decorated, making it comfortable," Marty said.

When he was abducted, he was wrapped in the comforter of that bed. No one thought anything about the comforter, but Marty always did. So, to put it all behind him, he went back to remodel and decorate that room as if it were his life's sole purpose. He found so much peace in just doing that: healing his inner spirit that had been broken for so long. In doing that, he was able to begin a relationship with his sister, who looked just like his mom. He had acted like she didn't exist for a minute. Dealing with that room was like dealing with his mother. He knew she would have been mad about the comforter, so he replaced it.

When he spent time with his sister on the weekends, they would have lunch or dinner inside that room, watching movies. At 15 years and seven months old, Marty was able to get a driver's permit, so he was able to drive, supposedly with a licensed driver. Since he was close to getting his license and so tall, however, he eased on by till he was 16 and able to get his license. As he got older, he got wiser, street-slick and street-hip to the game that never stops—one that sometimes is a blessing in disguise, they say, because things always could have been worse. The game can also be a curse that ends up with you and all your loved ones being locked up, whether physically, spiritually or emotionally!

THE GAME DON'T WAIT

Graduation Night For Empire Naughty Boy!

Although Naughty had already received his certificate, he was allowed to walk with his classmates, peers and friends across the stage to mark a milestone in his life. The girls had made it earlier that day, but they agreed to let their princesses get their beauty sleep in. With all their names having been called, with blue and gold all over the stage, they walked off and threw their hats in the air as is traditionally done at Casa Grande Union High School. Their family all attended the graduation, then went to Aunt Sha's house, where they had a feast for the young man. All the ladies pitched in a special dessert for each, which had the men feeling as though they were sitting on top of the world. Since the men had paid for everything, the girls had allowed the fellas to spend extra money on the tickets to the graduation. It sounds crazy, but it happened, making the fellas feel even more special.

As the lights of the night began to dim, they each set off

in different directions to execute their surprise to the fullest. First, Naughty and Daisha pulled up at a friend's house, who supposedly called and said to come right in. When they walked in, a group of their family members greeted them with, "Surprise!" Daisha looked at Naughty.

"I don't get it."

"Look around; then, you will."

He started leading her around, finding pictures of her all around the house. It was only when they got to their bedroom that it occurred to Daisha this would be their home. She screamed so loudly that everyone rushed in again, saying, "Congratulations!" Daisha faced Naughty and kissed him, then jumped into his arms and kissed him again. Once that was done, Naughty was to call Sheriff so he could come over to his friend's house with his girl, where there was another group to surprise them.

"Surprise!" Right away, Dulce caught on. She shyly thanked him and whispered in his ear something in Spanish, then gave him a kiss. Everybody joined in as they walked from room to room.

When others got to TJ's friend's house, his friend had told him to go on in and have a seat. He was at the store. There wasn't anything anywhere in the house to lead Teka to believe anything. Yet, five minutes after they sat down, there was a knock at the door. At first, the knock was exceptionally light.

Then, each subsequent knock became even louder until the crowds from the other houses busted inside the door as if they were police officers, saying, "Surprise!"

When the other girls asked, "Do you like your house?" Teka replied, "What do you mean?"

TJ said, "Babe, this is our home." Teka's mouth was hanging open, but her mother, Aunt Sharon, was thanking TJ and hugging her. She still couldn't believe it, until they went into their bedroom, where they were greeted with rose pedals strewn everywhere, candles lit and 10 bottles of white wine being chilled. Turning on the lights to open the bottles and grab all the fine China glasses, Teka was able to see a mirage of pictures of them from the beginning of their relationship. Teka then turned, kissed TJ and said, "Thank you." Once all the wine was passed out and everyone was feeling themselves, they all headed back to Aunt Sha's house, where they all ended up crashing all over the house. From that next day on, life would become chaotic as they rehearsed the wedding multiple times, allowing each bride to walk beautifully to the arms of their husbands from their fathers.

Teka hadn't seen her father and still thought him to be locked up, so they had TJ's brother, Tommy Jr., walk her down the aisle during rehearsal. On her special day, however, TJ flew her father into town for the wedding, and even had himself for and a tuxedo in advance to participate in the occasion. Each girl's father would walk them to the arms of their future husbands. On their special day, they had arranged for Teka to go last to avoid spoiling the surprise. Through one door came Tommy Jr., asking Teka if she was ready, with her responding, "As ready as I'll ever be." Tommy Jr. then led her into the room where her right of passage to holy matrimony would begin. As "Here Comes the Bride" began to play, from behind, without Teka having seen him, her father asked, "May I have the honor?" Teka thought she was tripping and became a bit discombobulated momentarily until it registered that her father was speaking to her. She screamed, which surely got everybody's attention. Some had caught on to the fact that this was her father, as others remained confused till after the wedding.

Teka quickly gathered her wits and moved on with the process, crying the whole way down the aisle. She placed her hand inside of TJ's, gave him a hug, and walked off. Teka was still crying as she looked into TJ's eyes, silently making promises to God, expressing thanks and reverence to her Heavenly Father for to her soon-to-be husband. Tears of joy began to fall from all three couple's eyes because they knew they were blessed and could've been put in jail for a long time—or, like Raheem and Man Man, resting in the bosom of their master. That day was very emotional for each one of them. Each family member came to greet them, starting with Tracy, who blessed them with forgiveness, wished them the best and reminded them not to forget about Days Transitional

Housing for God's People.

Thanks to her father and their lawyer, Arthur Sanders, they were blessed to have business prosper in legal ways. Arthur stepped up just during their trying and troubled time. Luscious Bell stepped up for each of them—she always did. No matter how troubled her life was, they knew they could always depend on her. Tyrik and Lil Mama then stepped up, as they were reminded of where Tyrik now stood in their lives. He had loved and supported Lil Mama in reciprocation of all she had given him in the past, and they all embraced him as a part of their future, adding and accepting him into the family. He loved Miss Charlesetta for her prayers and her love.

He appreciated her even more for her devotion to Sheriff and Naughty; she used to babysit them and feed them at her table. She continued to blessed them, just like she always did. Regarding Aunt Sha and Aunt Sharon, they let them know through their actions that forgiveness is everything—unless you forgive, you can't be forgiven. With Lady and Sweet Dreams Tracy, they learned that no matter what, friend who pray together stay together, and love is unconditional. With Marty stepping up, the revelation they each received is that love heals anybody and everything. If Marty could do it, so could they, together, as one big family.

Although Big Girl wasn't there, she was thought of. They were reminded not to take love, living or their freedom for granted; to always be there for their family members no matter what! After all, those who stepped up were repeated attractions throughout their lives that would contribute to their legacies. Abdul and Lety reflected true love by remaining abstinent until marriage, making it through to a solid foundation with the belief that love would keep them grounded for the century. Everyone agreed that Cupid had surely done his thing with all four of the couples. The next day, Uncle Arthur called up Luscious Bell.

"Hello?"

"Good afternoon, Ms. Luscious Bell. How are you after that grand old feast of marriage?" Arthur asked.

"I am doing good! As a matter of fact, I am blessed! My baby son and daughter-in-law are their way to Rome, Italy; they're off to their honeymoon. Hopefully, you're calling to let me know that."

"Yes, ma'am. You are no longer married to Mr. Sea; we just need to go through with your signatures. I'll notarize the documents, then we'll be done. Easy as that!"

"Are you and Gladys still at Sha's house?"

"Yes, we are. Would you like to stop by?" Arthur replied.

"That's fine, Arthur. I'm on my way. See you in a few!" Luscious Bell said.

"Will do!"

Aunt Sha and Aunt Sharon had been cooking brunch after everyone woke up past noon. Everyone was just lounging around the house, enjoying the company of one another. Miss Charlesetta, Tyrik and Lil Mama had also stayed at Aunt Sha's house because they had drank, then played dominoes, spades and Tunk. They all listened to oldies, but goodies, until the early parts of the morning. Like any other celebration, this one would go on all night, starting after they ate. Kids were already out on the back porch; some were swimming in the ground pool Aunt Sha had in her backyard. Tyrik, Lil Mama, Lady and Sweet Dreams were playing dominoes. Tracy and her husband, Elijah, were playing spades with Hollywood and Chi-Town. They were getting whooped by Hollywood and Chi, who were always a good team. All the little kids were running around, happy to see all the cousins and friends they hadn't seen since the family reunion in 2015.

Luscious Bell walked in and said, "Y'all didn't hear my knock?"

"No, ma'am," Aunt Sha said. "Come on 'round and grab a plate! We not gon' accept 'no' for an answer! Our children done went and jumped the broom. We not tired of celebrating that with each other!" Aunt Sha said.

"Excuse me! Bring that plate here, then!"

"Grandma?" Lil Mama and Tyrik's twins ran over to give Luscious Bell hugs and kisses.

"Hello, Lil and Big! Girls, how are you ladies doing?"

"Fine," they said in unison.

"I missed you, Grands," Lil said.

"Me, too!" Big said as she jumped in her grandma's lap, and the other followed.

"Lil and Big, let your Grands eat first!" Lil Mama said.

"At home, you the mama, but right now, let me be the Grands! Ya hear?"

"Luscious Bell, I'm glad you said that, 'cause that must mean I have a wonderful babysitter tonight!"

"I don't know about all that. I might have a date tonight!"

"I hope it ain't that midget again!" Lil Mama said. Everybody started laughing.

"Well, I might want to celebrate the divorce!"

"Yeah, right!!" Lil Mama laughed.

Luscious Bell ate a plate of food with both her granddaughters in her arms while talking to the other family members at the same time. Before she knew it, her babies were knocked out by time she finished eating. So, she laid them on the other side of her so they would know their Grands was still right here! Luscious Bell was overjoyed—ecstatic, really—when she heard the squeals of her grandbabies! She was so happy to see and embrace them because it had been a couple of weeks since they last called her.

She would be taking them home with her for a week or two. She figured Lil Mama and Tyrik needed a break, too. Charlesetta, Aunt Sha, Aunt Sharon, Tyrik and Lil Mama had planned to meet Mary and Exa V at the casino. Arthur and Sam were staying back to watch the game. Sam was just getting off at Francisco Grande Resort. Arthur, called "Funny Man" by Sam, was waiting to play the winners at domino table. Aunt Sharon eased out back to clean the grill and get it started, but she really wanted to smoke a joint. Marty had been flossing since he got back to the Grande. Since he got his Jaguar, he had been doing even better in school and work.

In Casa Grande, he played the Bad Boy role as he hung around his little Blood cousins. So, on the slick, he was a banging eastside Blood gangster. He'd rather bang than must get jumped in the set like Lil Damu wanted to do in Phoenix. Nobody in the family had a problem with wearing red or blue, which was crazy, because there were no Bloods or Crips in the family—"where they do that at!?" Everywhere generally remained quiet, but somehow, since the Bloods versus Cuz came out, the family didn't have them warring against each other. Now, they would almost kill each other over a girl or boy. So, the gang-banging was really an out-of-town thing, meaning when Big Gigg (Rest In Peace), Jeff, Sammy Dee, Peete, Ketchup, Damu or Moe Blood came through, that's the type of time these dudes were on. They're the ones who started that gangsta split, although the family experienced fatalities as members stepped out of town.

So, Marty first became famous in "Da Grande" by his own right, then known later as the son of the "Goddess of the WNBA." When he was in Phoenix, he played a good, on-the-slick hood boy. On Facebook, Monospace and Myspace, "Bad Boy," AKA Marty, was in many girls' ears, so he slowly but surely became "that dude". His main girl was Alissa, who was about that cash in a real way. She liked to smoke weed, and Bad Boy loved being around her, so she started keeping that dro on her, and eventually, he started blowing with her. She lived in Grande.

She reminded him of his father, and she was crazy like his mama—she had it like *that*! So, Bad Boy made it his business to hit the freeway to Da Grande in a hot minute, ducking and dodging Smokey the Bandit in real ways. Eventually, he became known for the good dro he had been getting from Ese Homez, who was a Blood, too, and kicked it with Bad Boy in Phoenix. He met him at the birthday party of his godfather, Cresta. From then on, they were like cousins; "primo" is what they called each other. There was nothing they wouldn't do for one another—thick as thieves!! If you had a problem with one, you had a problem with the other! Since his girl smoked the best, the trips to Da Grande became assets. The trips were no longer liabilities because the game came to him on a silver platter!

Ese Homez was M&M's nephew, whose Pop was supplied by M&M. This was unknown to Bad Boy because Ese knew how M felt about his godson. When they started raking in money, Ese wanted to approach his tío, M, but doing that would expose Bad Boy. That would be a problem. After some serious thinking, Ese decided to hit up Bad Boy the next time they planned to kick it. This would be sooner, rather than later, because these dudes were trying to put Da Grande on the map and cash in their pockets.

So, when Marty, AKA Bad Boy, met up with his *primo* and business partner, Ese, they started in on how to get that paper, then fall back. So, after blowing a couple of blunts, Ese got to the matter at hand.

"Primo," Ese said to Marty.

Marty had picked up on Spanish, talking as if he were Mexican, speaking it and understanding it all the same, but he was Black.

"You want to make some *feria*, right? So, yes, man," Marty said.

"*Tienes un problemo*: M. One problem: M."

Marty looked up quickly, as if he had just been stolen from! Just hearing the name of his *padrino*, M&M, was a threat—not just to him, but to anybody who crossed a line regarding his godson. Everybody knew the whole situation: how it all went down with Big Girl and how her last days played out. So, they knew that for every action, there would be a reaction. M&M had gotten back into the game after his wife passed away. Between his wife's death and Big Girl's death, he fell back into the game, playing third base if he had to for his big brothers. Yet, he was in retirement mode, so, "*No es Petho Carnal*," they would say. After he mourned his wife respectfully, he stepped up to the plate like he never left even more, as vicious as a rattlesnake! His big brothers nicknamed him "Tiberon," which means "shark"—a man-eater!

"What about him?" Marty asked.

"I am not going to keep disrespecting him, nor should you. We have to take this issue to him now, before we cross ourselves out the game," Ese said.

"You're right, *Primo*! *Vamose*!!! "Marty said. So, Marty AKA Bad Body, and Ese headed to his *tío*'s house, lettering themselves in with the key.

"Whoa! *Primo*, what are you doing?" Ese exclaimed.

"You said we were gonna go talk to my *padrino*!"

"I'm talking about the key and walking in! *Cálmate*, Ese! "

They headed to the backyard, where Marty's *padrino*, M&M, was in his backyard with Lawrence, who had all kinds of roosters of his own. He also had some killer dogs, a diamond in the rough as his woman, two sons, and, yes, that nice Silverado!

Without even looking back, M said, "¿Que pasa, mijos?"

"*Necesita hablando contigo.*"

"¡Sabes que siempre tengo tiempo para ti, con todo lo que haces por mí, sobrino! ¿Qué sucede?" M&M replied to his nephew.

"*Nada. ¿Como estas, Tío?*"

"*Todo bien, tu sabes.* That's how I do it, Ese!" M&M said, giving his nephew some love.

"*Mijos*, go ahead and talk. Lawrence is *mi hermano.*"

"Tío, I've been disrespecting you by selling weed, but I've been making a few dollars!"

"*Mijo*, that doesn't surprise me at all. I knew that one day, you would be in the game, because the game is like bullets—it has no name."

Lawrence and Ese went off, chasing one of the roosters that had gotten loose. They were trying to whip the other ones, and they'd fight till they were dead! With them both being gone, M&M was able to address his concerns.

"¿Mijo, Bad Boy, *ey?*"

"Sí, Tio, "Marty said. He referred to his ghetto name. "*Soy Tiboron*! They call me that 'cause I'm worse that the shark, Jaws. He was always out for blood jaws and was a man-eater, and so I am! I'll kill as quick as Jaws and feed 'em to the

Marranos."

"*Mijo*, to be honest, I don't want you in the game, just like I didn't want your mama in the game, but I didn't have no say."

"Didn't you supply her, *Tío*? No disrespect; simply curious. I've always wondered about that, 'cause one plus one kept coming out to be more than two."

M&M had gotten quiet. At times, he felt responsible for her death, because he should've taken care of the situation himself and not taken Big Girl with him. He stood by the decision that he made and would tell himself, *The result would always have been the same, just with different people and times*. Having never lied to Marty, he knew he wouldn't start now.

"Yes, son, I did. But I'm not sorry at all because I couldn't stop her, but I did my darndest to protect her. That day, I had all the best Mafia killers in the world, with a ride-or-die chick who wasn't getting played for no money, let alone you, who was her life. I never knew or thought she would go upside dude's head like that, but she was worse than a mother protecting her cub. To top it off, it was the dude who was working for her. Your mother did what was necessary. To try to stop her, like trying to stop you, would be ludicrous! *Mijo*, I feel honored that you would come to me, so I know what type of time you on. Don't get it twisted for a moment, because the game doesn't wait for your mama—Rest In Peace. So, I'm telling you that I don't want this for you, or really condone it, but I'm gonna protect you in the game. No matter what you do in life, whatever game you choose to play, be the absolute best at it. The result is usually jail, prison or death. Many have felt they could change the game, even the rules, but the end result never changes… Somebody wins, somebody loses, and me? I play to win!"

M&M continued:

"Every move is strategic. You have to weigh your pros and cons and discuss these things with yourself before you step up to the plate to play:

Do I care that I could get killed?

How would those who love me feel?

I can end up in prison for life.

Do I want to put my loved ones at risk?

I'm doing the crime, but can I do the time?

Is this what I really want my life to consist of?

Is there a better way?

Is this an example I want to set for my children?

What about how my mom felt? What happened to her.?

Would my mom have wanted this life for me, or would she want better?

You must be able to deal with the consequences of what could be, or who you could possibly hurt, because when you get to jail or prison, you take your family there emotionally. These are some things you must think of—if not now, then later when you're in jail, in prison, or on your death bed as you fade out. GAME OVER!"

By then, Lawrence and Ese had caught the rooster, put a chain on its leg, and put it in the cage. Lawrence was drinking a Budweiser, and Ese was on Myspace, getting down and rapping with the homies.

"Just think about that, *Mijo.* Now *Sobrino,* what you need to holla at me about?" M said.

"Who said I wanted to talk to you?" Ese, said looking at Bad Boy.

"Don't look at me, little puppet!" Marty said and laughed. "I didn't say nothing."

Ese put the spill on M&M, and from there, Marty and Ese were doing their thing. They started from quarter grams of dro, then went to ounces, then on to the big league of pounds that ran down the I-10 Casa Grande exit like runaway slaves from the south! Dauphin County in Harrisburg, Pennsylvania, has the most overpopulated jails and prisons in the nation. Warehousing men had become a multi-billion-dollar organization. It's sad that they're building more jails and not worrying about rehabilitations. Instead of legalizing marijuana, they're selling more beer and wine, even moonshine.

Meanwhile, back at Da Grande, once Marty and Ese

kicked down the door to M&M's Fort Knox, they had it paid in the shade! From dro, they went on to drop crack or coke, then ecstacy pills, Percocets, Perc-30s, and oxycontin. Just like an ice cream parlor or a candy store, they had many flavors.

Marty was a senior in high school at South Mountain. He was doing incredibly good in school, getting A+ and O+ grades. He only went to school for half the day, then played basketball at South Mountain, and had many scouters watching him. In the beginning, it was appealing, but once that money started dropping like hot cakes on ole boy, his interest diminished.

Marty knew his *padrino* liked to come see him play; he even had hopes that he would be in the NBA. M&M never really said it, but he always insinuated who the Goddess was and how she got down. It is said good things come to those who wait. Big Girl had already signed the contract with the WNBA, even practicing for it. M&M also told Marty, AKA Bad Boy, that his mother never needed to hustle, but she got herself caught up trying to help ole girl and Raheem get lifted, only for dude to bite hand that fed him. M&M really didn't want to send his godson out into the streets, but he knew Marty had a better chance of surviving in the jungle if he could help him. Marty was like the son M never had; he was smart, Black and talented with skills to take over the court. Instead, he was choosing to monopolize the game and the streets, taking it all for granted. ALL MONEY AIN'T GOOD MONEY!

When it comes to choosing, think of winning, not losing! At the end of the day, ya boy be tired of looking back for either the police or somebody trying to bump his head for a couple of dollars. In the game, I admit, there were times when having the sack on me kept me lifted with paper, and even that natural high that made me feel like "that dude." Everybody loves that feeling, plus the come-up is like icing on the cake. But when the bullet hits the bone and you've been shot down with a bullet, or by the police, or even the stuck-up kid you been flossing and bossing in front of, it's not the greatest feeling by far when you hit the ground. Yet, we still take that chance, spinning the dice, thinking, *You only live once.* Not caring about the others, we involve them after the fact. When we out in those bricks, acting like Caroline, like our stuff don't stink, can't nobody tell us nothing! That is, until the bullet of reality has hit the bone. This is where we all find that jail talk and try paper pippin', playing ourselves, 'cause those people are hip to that game. We ain't the first ones to try to spin it!

I've had my good days in the game, and I'm still having bad days. 16 years later, Pennsylvania still wants my blood or my body. This fact is my motivation to stay focused on the prize of the higher calling in Christ, because he himself is the only one able to destroy the evil that lies behind these cases. Doing time gets no better. Actually, it's getting worse, because society's only solution is to lock us up like the animals we portray ourselves to be. They have given up on us, yet in forgetting about us, they're forgetting about themselves. Going to school at South Mountain, there were a lot of Bloods, as opposed to Crips, so that alone kept them all in a neutral zone. Playing different basketball teams at home or away, the competitiveness mixed with the red or blue colors that lie beneath explosions. These explosions, at times, would be handled off the court and in the bricks, often causing drive-bys at schools, malls and gas stations. During this time, Marty was going to school and dating a Chicana girlfriend. She was called "nigger lover" in Spanish, and a large amount of other racial names that led to many fights as well. On Marty's trips to Casa Grande, since he was a Blood, he had beef with Casa's north, east, and south sides. The fact that he had a Mexican girlfriend made it even worse. This often led to little shoot-outs. After killing my cousin, Deshawn (Rest In Peace), it got even worse, with both sides having the green light on each other. This became somewhat of a ripple effect throughout the Pinal County Detention Center, where they had riots that left a few close to death, if not dead.

Throughout the Arizona Department of Corrections and back to the streets, these wars continued, and eventually came and went in different seasons. Going from colors, red and blue, to Blacks versus Mexican/Chicano Crips, these different gangs now start on the prison guards and are then brought to the streets. Building more jails and persons may be becoming a multi-billion organization meant to warehouse men and women, but for gangs, these spaces are becoming their headquarters that will more than likely lead to… only heaven knows. Marty made it through his senior year, even graduating without incident. He held his graduation party in Da Grande, and it was made into a Blood party.

For Pinal County, to date, is all bad because the lawmakers are making examples out of those who they've targeted as clans of some kind. Although Bad Boy Marty had been scouted by many, he turned his back to them all, turning his game from the court to the streets. He never let his uncle, aunt or grandma see his hand of cards he was playing. They knew he was Bad Boy, the seed of Big Girl, yet he was unknown as the most hated, most feared, most thorough dude. The game don't wait!

After graduation, Marty, AKA Bad Boy and Ese started getting it how they lived—viciously in in the paint! They were earning higher than the people on top of the Empire State Building who did research on public knowledge. In posts, in the Gazette, and around the Philly area, they found the names and addresses of the people involved, as well as their children. Marty found his name amongst the massacre. He smiled and said, "Guerra!" Filling out college grant applications to go to school online was part of the plan to get free housing and make himself look good to whomever it may concern. Getting approved allowed Bad Boy an easy way to move into a townhome in Scottsdale, Arizona. Here, he could mix and mingle with those who chose to further their educations in the business world of literature while they served the streets of the business world. Being close to campus and, at times, having to utilize the facility during tests, they were able to meet their peers from different states during testing time. After the first semester, Bad Boy met Walah, who was from the north side of Philly. He was from 23rd and Diamond, and grew up in the Raymond Rose Projects that housed all Blacks. This neighborhood was definitely drug-infested, as well as roach-infested, and I can't tell you which one is worse!

"What the breezies looking like up that way? Yo! The chickens is straight," Walah said. "One of the times when it's really going down, you gonna have to let your boy sightsee the spring break festival that be going down in the college towns 'round my way." Walah was six feet, five inches tall, and Bad Boy was six feet, three inches tell. Walah used to play for Penn State College, but he was trying to get out of the city, so he took the first scholarship on the west coast in Phoenix, Arizona, at Mesa Community College. Walah was Muslim, and since Arizona had one of the largest populated mosques, similar to Sister St. Clair or the Nabawi Mosque Chapel he used to go to in Philly. Walah was very outgoing and funny, so fitting in with Baby Boy and Ese was easy. Yes, it was often straight-faced and straight-laced—"Firme Steelo" of a mad dog look. When Walah was in the mix, it was as if he was like magic, breaking frowns down and turnin' them around!

The role Ese was being finessed for was one that would one day replace M&M's, but as it's said, "There is no rest for the weary." He was too honorary to die too soon! So, this is why he had learned to always be serious. The position he would be given wouldn't call for soft hearts, only ones of the most vicious and ruthless. He had to be willing to take his momma out if she got out of pocket! For 12 hours, Tyrik had been trying to get in touch with Bad Boy, so when he did reach him, he had an attitude.

"Where you been?!"

"Whoa, what you mean, 'where I've been'?" Marty hung up. Since Bad Boy was already headed to the gym, he didn't answer when Tyrik called him back. Since Ese was with him, he had an image to uphold and didn't want anybody to disrespect his gangster. So, he bucked back on Tyrik—come correctly at your boy! Walking into the gym and into the office to go over to the books as he always did, Tyrik asked Ese to step outside.

"He don't need to step outside, Tyrik. Anything you say can be said in front of my family," Bad Boy said. Tyrik was thrown off by Bad Boy's attitude, but he pressed on with what he wanted to talk about.

"Marty, I went to cash my check, and it wouldn't clear," Tyrik said "Yeah, my bad," Marty said. "I had the accounts to where they would need my signature on them first. How much was it for?"

"1,867.63."

"What, you don't trust me, now? After all these years I've been working? It's nothing like that. It's just time I step up to the plate, you heard?"

"I feel you. My bad for tripping; it's just that when them white people was looking me all upside down, your boy Rogahn left me feeling some type of way!" Tyrik said. "Right, right." You good… this time. Next time, I'll have to cut you," Marty laughed.

Finishing up there, Bad Boy went next door to talk to Lil Mama, who was doing her homework for her last semester in business management.

"Lil Mama, I almost had to take your man's head off for coming at me sideways 'bout me changing the check cashing policy. Need my John Henry on the account just to step up and take the weight off Tyrik," Bad Boy said.

"He told me you could have at least let him know, 'cause many of the times, he had worked for free for the better of the team and for you," she said. "My bad, Auntie," he said, and just walked out, feeling like he didn't need to explain himself about something that belonged to him. Yeah, he did feel a little bad, since he seen in the books that he had only started on the payroll last year. Bad Boy's phone beeped and when he looked at it he saw a Facebook friend request from "Sapphire."

Sapphire—the name alone was intriguing eno-ugh to skip the mess he was dealing with. Clicking on to accept the request, he saw a sexy, brown-skinned woman with the Jada Pinkett Smith hairdo, around five-foot-seven, with the face and body of Trina, the baddest chick! Marty accepted that jawn off rip. From there, your boy was digging deep in that thing, looking at flicks of her and her Puerto Rican mommy friend. If it wasn't so sinful and greedy, like Bad Boy would have wanted to grip on both those GPs! Keeping chivalry alive, he scratched that thought and decided he would be kind enough to spin that thing in Ese's direction to keep it G.

So, he copied the photo, then placed it on the back-burner for Ese. After going through Sapphire's pictures he was not only intrigued, but terribly impressed to have come upon such a gem so unique. Believe it or not, she was a one of a kind, porcelain-like, a handcrafted Black Barbie doll-looking thing. She had Bad Boy's situation out of control, to the point he had to thaw out one of the rain checks he had on ice! Spinning a few things off to get his mind right with Frieda, who always had just what the boy needed, he went on about his day. He had to hit that E-way to the Grande to drop a few bombs to keep that cheddar in motion. The freeway wasn't busy at all, so Bad Boy got there in no time. Listening to a few jams on the box had him feeling like himself as he thought of where he was, where he had been and where he wanted to go. His life had changed dramatically in so many ways after his mother passed away. The things they used to talk about—her hopes and dreams that she used to share with him, so full of life, love and safety—seemed to have disappeared into total nothingness. Through her eyes, he had built an empire of love and security. When she passed, so did that empire. It took him a few years to find a foundation solid enough for him to build on. Storms of many kinds had seemed to continue to blow his way, causing him to fall down, only to get right up and try again. Eventually, he found a ground worth tilling, creating a foundation for, and finally building on. Some days were easier than the last. He experienced many rough days thereafter, but day by day, he began getting stronger, with a desire to live, learn and love. With the help of his *padrino*, his life begin to have meaning, because everything his *padrino* did would be for the better of him. Seeing that his life and light were shown in various ways began to motivate and inspire him to become who he needed to be for himself.

Naughty and Asia had found the souls of their very own in each other. Deja couldn't get enough of his soft and sweet, yet aggressive kisses or lovemaking. Every touch of Naughty had become very hypnotic, always leaving her in a dreamlike state that continuously had her sitting on top of the world. She couldn't get enough of him, nor could he get enough of her; they would end up making love for hours, getting lost in each other's eyes. If the eyes were truly windows to the soul, each found that bright beacon of life that would always lead them home—a light that even time could never dim by far. The love, peace and joy that they found in their lovemaking was built on love, honor, trust and loyalty that would be a ripple effect for many generations to come. At times, Sherriff and Dulce couldn't believe they had climbed a mountain of love together. If he wasn't pinching her, she was pinching him, so each would know this night would last throughout their lives and forevermore.

When the devil, in his craftiness, would try to penetrate these foundations of love, he would always fail. Man could not destroy what God put together. Having built their houses on stable foundations, they knew that no matter what storms may come their way, they would be anchored in and not move an inch. They knew that in life and love, as a whole, each would be willing to sacrifice. They kept lines of communication clear so their love would never hunger or thirst; as one, they now had a river of life flowing through their garden of love. Each would be watchful of the evil weeds that must be uprooted and destroyed to keep the garden of harvest fruitful, as God promised this legacy. TJ and Teka took long walks through the city of love. Everything was as beautiful, just as their life would be. Everywhere they looked, it all reminded them of the blessing of God's creation and His purpose.

"Honey, this is how I always want us to be. I've heard of many things other couples had been through, but those things could never come our way. TJ, for the rest of our lives, I will remain the woman you desire to become your wife; to love, cherish and honor. If not, I'll become better." "My brown-skinned queen, there isn't a mountain I wouldn't move for you, nor river, lakes or oceans that couldn't be swam for you, nor waves of trouble we couldn't surf. Our love will always remain as pure as snowflakes. My love will always be as full as the clouds in the sky. Our love will be always as attentive as it is today. Teka, I thank you for your love, for your promise that reaches my soul. You fill me up with fire in the night. I will always respect you and treat you as my queen. Our life will forever be a honeymoon."

In the midst of Bad Boy doing his thing, spreading his hustle and spinning Da Grande like a yo-yo, Sapphire popped up on Facebook Messenger.

"What up, yo?!" Sapphire said. "Holla at ya, God!" Bad Boy said.

"Thanks for your acceptance." "It's a pleasure—an honor—to have a gem such as yourself in my zone, Boo."

"...'Boo'? Do you accept to all females? Are they 'Boo,' too?" "Nah, I'm not even on that type of time. I feel like you're special. Thought I must give homage to such a gem as yourself," Bad Boy said. She responded, "Why, thank you! Now, you got my tongue tied and my wheel spinning for a comeback."

"Say no more... Just tell me about your life, 'cause mine is real." "I'm 17, I'll be a senior this upcoming year, and I'm a virgin."

"Whoa! Yo! You out of pocket," he said. "Nah, G. That there is real... I got good P all day, with pounds of self-respect." "I feel you, Ma. When a name is sweet like yours, that tells me you come with a gang of sass, too! Ma, let me hit you later. I gotta handle this business and head back to college. Have a good day, and keep doing you," Bad Boy said. "That's cool. Be safe, yo," Sapphire said.

Bad Boy was already in his feelings—not about her, but about himself, 'cause that conversation left him lifted above the stars. Surely, she would one day be his angel. When he finished handling his situations in the Grande, he went by his grandma's house. When he pulled up in her driveway, he saw the front screen door open and the TV on, and he vaguely heard his grandma singing gospel. He eased into the side door; the sprinkler was on by the front door, so she always kept the screen door locked. His grandma was singing "God Never Fails," and as she sang, she embraced him.

As he walked deeper into the house, he said, "Grandma, I love you." "Marty, I love you, too," she said as she gave him the much-needed hug. Their eyes filled with tears as they hugged each other tightly. "Son, I was just thinking about you," she said. "You mean praying for me, right?" he laughed.

"All the same. Cut the sass, young man! U-Haul

Green, come on in here and have a bite. Let your grandma fuss over you. Come here. Let me see how much taller you've gotten. You're growing like a tree now! Just 'cause you done got your Pa Pa's height don't mean you grown or you can whoop me, 'cause I can still throw down better than the best of 'em! So, come around, have a seat and rest your feet," Luscious Bell said. She had been praying for him and praising the Lord. Luscious Bell was tickled pink as she said, Thank you, Father. You are humorous and surprising, as usual." She was speaking to God as if He had been standing right beside her, opening up the refrigerator, putting plates in the microwave and pulling them right on out in 15 minutes. He knew Bad Boy would come to his grandma's house.

Marty watched her, admiring her while she thanked God for blessing him with the woman who always asked questions. She knew the answers as she left for work. In her soul, she felt that his spirit was low, and she wanted him to know that his grandma still loved him the same. He knew he could always show up here, and those arms would be open wide, ready to embrace him and protect him from all the evils of the world. Coming there was like being in paradise. He ate, and before he could even get up, she had prepared the sweetest pecan pie with his favorite, butter pecan ice cream, slightly melted over it. To top it off, she poured him a large, ice-cold glass of Carnation whole milk that made it all hit the spot. His grandma was always cleaning up and piddling around in the kitchen. Marty got up, went to the living room and changed the channel to Judge Judy. He ended up knocked out on the couch. His grandma got a sheet and covered him up, just like she would when he was smaller.

"Hey, little dude! What you doing sleeping on my mom's couch? I can't even stretch out on here like you doing. She'll run me out of here!" Lil Mama said. Marty looked, around gathering his thoughts and remembering where he was. As he looked out the screen door that was still open, he noticed it was dark outside. He looked at the clock; it was 7:45 p.m. He laughed, feeling better than he had in a long time. His little cousins were running around. Tyrik and Tommy Jr. were outside shooting, while Lil Mama, Miss Charlesetta and his grandma were in the kitchen talking. In the next few minutes, he dozed off again, awakening to his grandma setting a big plate of fried chicken, mashed potatoes, gravy, creamed corn and cornbread on a dinner tray. *It's almost as if she's putting a bib on me, getting ready to feed me as she did when I was a child*, he thought. The feeling was one of so much love, peace and happiness that almost made him want to come home for good.

When he finished eating, his uncle and Tyrik were heading in after playing under the streetlight that seemed to call every kind of bug—mosquitoes, flies and everything else. He got up, taking his plate that was so spotless you would have thought he licked it clean, to the kitchen. He washed it and rinsed it, just as he was taught. Looking outside, he noticed his car going automatically. He knew his grandma had it. He didn't care where she went 'cause he knew she just didn't want him to leave yet. Walking into his grandma's home was like walking into a pure, bright light. All the darkness of his life would light up, letting him know this was where he needed to be. However, coming back home definitely exposed his true self, 'cause if nobody knew him, Grandma did! She pulled his cards quicker than God got the news! *Ain't that the truth*, Marty thought as he grabbed his phone and turned it on. His grandma wanted all the attention, and she would get it. When Marty turned that phone on, it played so many tunes that he forgot it had four different alerts. He found that Al issa had hit him up:

"Who's driving your car? I followed them to the church, and now they sitting in there, talking. How you playing me?"

He responded, "Girl, go ahead and run up on that car like you got a problem. Luscious Bell and her crew gon' have you satisfied, then crucified and sporadically placed on the cross!" Marty said. He busted out laughing.

"Oh, that's your grandma! Hey, Miss Luscious Bell! I didn't know that was you. I'm sorry; I thought it was Marty."

In the background, Lisa said, "Let me find out you wanted to go a couple with Luscious Bell," and walked off. Marty was fit to be tired as he began laughing so hard that he cried and his stomach hurt.

"So, Bad Boy, how long are you down here for?" Alissa asked.

"Till tomorrow, but I need to spend a few minutes with my grandma. So, wait till I hit you up, 'cause she don't play with the phone thing! I was trying to slide up on you, but after she made me a plate, I dozed off." "Um, I miss you." "Ditto," he said. For so long, she had been trying to bring some goo goo gaga into the mix, but when she did, he bent a corner on her—literally! "I'll hit you, though, Alissa!" That's cool. Call me then. I'll be out and about." "Right."

He was on a mission to get at Sapphire. He looked online, and there she was.

"What do you do, Ma?! I've been meaning to ask you, how did our paths cross?" Bad Boy asked. "Whoever you recently added as a friend had to be a friend of mine, 'cause I'm in Philly and you're somewhere in… Arizona? Is that how you say it?" "Yes, it is." So, more than likely, she had known Walah.

They kept texting back and forth, then he had a Skype message all of a sudden. He opened it, and it was Sapphire live talking on Skype! It was fun, so he promised they would do it again, then told her he had to study for exams. "Are you a nerd?" she asked next. "Where in the devil you get that from?!" "This is the second time you spoke of school." "Well, ya boy gotta put that thing sitting on his shoulders to use! That's how I get D!" "Okay, okay. I can dig it, yo! Let me not hold you up. Hit me up when you want to talk. It's nice to talk to you." "You, too! We definitely gonna keep in touch."

"Later!" she said. "ONE!" Bad Boy said. Luscious Bell walked in and they talked for an hour. She then headed to her room and gave him a hug.

"Thank you for coming to see me. You made my day! You growing on up, and your momma would be so proud of you! Don't you leave here without giving your grandma a hug and kiss. Hopefully, that'll last till the next blue moon when you come through again." "I won't, Grandma, Marty said. She went into her room and closed the door. The moment he figured she was asleep, he hit the streets on Da Grande. Like an alley cat, he crept through, picking up his money at all the spots. He made his drops; everyone had his dough.

With the last few drops, it was almost as if these dudes were trying to play him 'bout his money. But now, from the looks of things, it was all a misunderstanding. He told each one of the curb-serving dudes when he came back, though, since his price let them make sure that they would have their own paper when they called again. This could work for them to come up in a real way. To all, it sounded like a plan. He pulled through the west side, where Alissa, Cosetta, Monica and Mercedes were kicking it outside with Chad, who had a few items he was slinging.

"What's up, Bad Boy?! I got the..."

He was trying to say his piece before Bad Boy hit him wit', "Nigga,I don't mess wit' you!" And as soon as Chad heard that click-clack, he was in the win, 'cause word had it that Bad Boy's name was what it was for a real reason. All games aside, Bad Boy wanted to make an example out of somebody! Alissa hopped in the whip, then he spun it off to his grandma's house and pumped on her for a minute.

"You hungry?" he asked. He was ready to bounce now that he had some leg in his money.

"Yes, I am," she said.

"Wait for me in the car so I can tell my grandma I'm bouncing." Heading out to the car, she felt some type of way about how he had been getting down with her lately, hitting it and then bouncing. The more she thought about it, the more upset she became. When he finally made it to the car with two plates of food, she got excited—that is, till she saw Luscious bell behind him. Luscious Bell opened up the door for him, looked in and gave her a look, saying, "Mm-hmm." Alyssa fell back and lost her appetite. She was heated again. As soon as Marty pulled off, he felt her looking all upside his head like she wanted to take it off!

"Yo! What's the biz?! Why you muggin' me like dat?!"

"I'm just feeling some type of way 'cause all you do is pump and go like I'm a gas station of some kind!"

"If that's how you feel, say no more. Let's do us both a solid and end it," Bad Boy said. She said to herself, *He just went there, didn't he?!* From that moment on, she knew there would be no dispute of any kind, nor was there reason to say anything more. He dropped her back off at the spot, and as soon as the door closed, he was gone , never to look back. Looking back is for suckers who are begging to be mistreated 'cause they are gluttons for punishment. He would never be that dude! Bad Boy hit the freeway and was at his apartment sooner than he knew it. He got his papers out of his console, added to others and then headed in.

Ese was sitting at the table, counting money and bagging up pounds for the next drops. Bad Boy sat down and counted his set with the wap that Ese had stacked up. Danny started bagging up 'cause they never kept anything in the crib—surely not two bales! Four hours later, calls had been made, and out the door they were till the early morning. As soon as they got home and their heads hit the pillows, they were out like a light with their pockets full! When the alarm came on, without a snooze button to press, Bad Boy had to get right on up and turn it off. Then, he headed to the restroom and found his gat was cocked! It hurt so badly that he could barely stand up; he had to hold onto his gat, only letting a little bit of pee out at a time! "I'm gonna kill this girl!" was all he could say after he looked at his boxers. They were full of pus that was almost as colorful as the rainbow! It seemed like the more urine he let out, the worse the pain got; it felt like knives were shooting out. The last squeeze he let out hurt the most, knocking him to his knees. Bad Boy hit the ground so hard it woke up Ese, who ran into the bathroom.

"¿Que pasa, Primo? What's wrong?!" Ese asked.

"The girl I've been pumping on burned me! Better yet, she cooked me!" Bad Boy said, in excruciating pain he almost couldn't bear.

"¿Por que tu no usar un condom?" Ese asked. ¡No lo sé, Primo! Por qué ? ¡Loco!" Bad Boy said. He wanted to call her and pull her card, but he didn›t want her to give her the satisfaction. That was the first time he had ever ridden without a saddle. Now, his horse was down and his gun jammed! He had been so nervous, thinking he was gonna get caught up when he bared that thing back—now, he really had a situation! When he did finally decide to get at the girl, he was really gonna be sick! For now, he was just bumping music, going to school and going straight to the clinic to cite and release whatever STD he had! When he got to the health clinic, it seemed like everyone he knew was there. WHY?! They were all suspiciously looking at each other, like, "You got it, too?!" When they called him by name, Marty Lemons, it seemed like she yelled so loudly that it caused everybody to look his way, and it seemed like they all had smirks on their mugs .He went in to see the doctor and explaining his symptoms.

The doctor just laughed. "I'll be right back." It seemed

like the doctor was never coming back, when he did, he brought with him what looked like a turkey baster, with a needle as long as his arm.

"Bend over," the doctor said. "For what?!" Marty asked nervously, ready to run out the door. The doctor, a Black man, almost died laughing at this dude.

The whole time, Bad Boy wasn't as bad as he was supposed to be after looking at that needle. Once the doctor had piped him down a bit—let me rephrase that: settled him down a little bit—he was able to explain that he was giving him a shot of the highest dose of antibiotics on his lower hip. They would then wait on the results and take it from there.

The doctor then gave Marty the shot, which seemed to hurt just as badly as the STD; after almost passing out, Bad Boy made it through the that jawn. Then, the doctor left. 30 minutes later, in came two male nurses he knew for a fact were sweeter than cotton candy. He wondered what they were there for.

"Can I leave now?" Bad Boy asked. "Afraid not. Sir, you not only have one STD, but three: gonorrhea, chlamydia and syphilis! I hope it was worth it," one of the nurses said.

"What you mean?!" "Until this procedure is complete, you are to be quarantined. If you leave, we have to call the police, because you are toxic," the nurse said. "Really?"

"Really, sir. May we proceed?" In his mind ,these dudes seemed gayer and gayer by the minute. There was no way he wanted these Froot Loops all on his tip—literally! So, to test his own flame, as well his security in himself as a man, he went ahead and let them work on his gun. He said to himself, *At least they'll take good care of it!*, and laughed out loud. When it was all said and done, these nurses were thorough, effective and professional at all times. He viewed those who lived alternative lifestyles with respect as people, not as ass eaters. *Judge and ye shall be judged...* In life, as many dangers, toils and snares are tossed in the way of many, you never know what the people you deal with every day have been through or how they ended up being who or what they are today.

Talking about these people could have you chasing your own tail, and could these be the very same people to help you when everyone else has given up on you. A wise one has said, "Love thy neighbor as you love yourself, for God is love." Treat people the way you want to be treated. Who's to say you could have possibly been entertaining God's angel? Hours later, when the percocets wore off, Bad Boy felt everything they did with that long Q-tip to clean him out. He felt disgusted by his bad case of love and the way he had gotten caught slipping on his pimping. He was mad; he wanted to call her and verbally annihilate her character, then disrespect her like the dirty dog he felt like. He had a straight "eat that and take it for the team" mentality. Feeling like a lost, beaten puppy, he went to M&M's house.

After letting himself in, heading through the unusually quiet house and looking around, something just didn't seem right. So, he backtracked through the house in the same way he came—that was when he saw his godfather laying there. Quickly checking his pulse, he found it to be weaker than one usually is, so he dialed 9-1-1.

Inside, he began to panic because he didn't want to lose his *padrino* now or ever. He loooked through the house to make sure all was in one piece, as it was to be. In the past, M&M had spoken to his godchild about what to do in case of an emergency. Because his son and grandchildren were all Christians, there were things he didn't want to expose to the others. Out of loyalty and precaution, before he headed to the door, he went through the motions once again. All was well, so he headed to the door. As he opened it, the paramedics were coming up the walkway. Leading the way as if it were the Battle of Jericho, he led them to his *padrino*, then began to pray.

The EMS began to work on him, getting an IV, blood and more ready en route to the hospital. Marty said he would follow in the car. On his way, he called Ese, and then his godbrother and grandkids, to meet him at Saint Joseph's Hospital. In less than 30 minutes, all except Ese were present, awaiting to hear from the doctor. Marty's godbrother led them all into prayer, asking for God's will to be done.

"Hello. I'm Doctor Mutap. Mr. M was suffering from a severe diabetic attack."

"Diabetic?" M&M's family asked in unison. "Apparently, he couldn't have known, nor is it anywhere in his file from his doctor. We're running more tests to be sure that is all. He is heavily medicated at this point in time, so to ensure he gets rest, we've heavily sedated him," the doctor said. "When can we see him?" his son asked. "You're welcome to see him for five minutes. Then, till morning, he will need complete rest after suffering from a close diabetic coma. He'll remain in the ICU till morning. If you give us a number, we'll call you," the doctor said.

Marty stopped the doctor right then and there. "Sir, I'm not leaving his side!" He said it in such a authorititative voice he had to look around; it was as if his godfather had said it. It was fully understood what was going down. Marty knew M&M's godbrother had his kids and his sister's kids, and that he had to get home. "Rene, what you want to do is up to you, but I'll be here. I'll keep you informed if you choose to go. I know you have the kids." "That's fine, Marty, and thank you," Rene said.

"No need to thank me; no need to thank me. I love my *padrino*," Marty said, looking Rene in his eyes. Rene had always been somewhat jealous of the relationship his dad and Marty had. He used to call his dad "nigger lover"

74

until his dad told him that hating Marty was a sin. The Holy Spirit had deeply connected with Rene, to the point that Rene apologized to Marty. Marty had truly forgiven him, because this forgiveness was for him, not for Rene. In order to be forgiven, you have to be willing to forgive, period. From that moment on, the healing process began for both of them.

Ese made it to the hospital after a while. *"How's my tío?"* "He's better. He almost went into a diabetic coma, but he made it on time. *Gracias Dios* Rene came, and his kids, too, but the doctor said he'll be asleep till morning," Bad Boy said.

"Let me call my dad, then, and let him know." "Cool." Marty knew he had to let Ese know about his "issues," meaning his STD, because Ese was like a brother to him. "My dad said he'll be here in the morning. Are you all right?" "Yeah, I went to the clinic and got my situation handled. It's all good now," Bad Boy said.

The doctor was heading home and he saw Marty was still there. He also knew Marty was worried, so he stopped by and gave them five minutes to see M&M: "He's doing better. You can go see him for five minutes." "Thanks," they said, and together, they went in to see M&M. After the five minutes were up, they headed back out to the ICU waiting room.

"Marty, I'll be heading home soon, but I'm going across the street to get you something to eat. You want anything else?" Ese asked. He was getting ready to say no, but then it occured to him that he needed antibiotics the doctor hafd prescribed to him. "Sí, mon! Can you get my prescription filled at Walgreens?" "I sure can, since you woke up yelling and fussin' and carrying on. What did you stick your dick in?" ESE said as he laughed and headed out. He knew Bad Boy wanted to choke him for that; he probably would have if somebody else wasn't around. Ese knew better than to cross the line. While Ese was gone, Marty, AKA Bad Boy, fell into a deep sleep. He started dreaming about his mom. She would always be fighting Raheem in his dream. Then, he would walk around the corner, hear the gunshot and wake up screaming.

That's how Ese found him when he brought his food. They lived together and were like brothers, so he would always come in and start telling him in Spanish to wake up. He knew the Spanish would trigger his memory and confuse him, letting him know he was dreaming.

"¡Carnal! Tu suenos, no sirven!" This meant, "Brother, your dreams aren't good! Wake up!"

Bad Boy's eyes opened suddenly. Then, he sat up quickly.

"¿Que pasa?" Bad Boy asked.

"*Primo*, you were dreaming. Here take these and eat, 'cause you can't take them on an empty stomach. Are you coming home?" Ese replied.

"No, I'm staying with my *padrino*," he said. Any other

time, Ese would've had his clown suit on, but he wouldn't touch this with a 10-foot pole!

"¡Orale, Primo! I'm out. Get some sleep, and *no más sueños malos*!" Ese said, meaning, "No more bad dreams!"

When Ese left, Bad Boy finished eating. Then, he began to nod off, and the nurse walked in.

"You could sleep in the room with your *padrino*," she said.

He jumped up and followed the nurse, watching the sway of her hips the whole time. She must have felt his eyes burning holes in her scrubs, 'cause she turned around and caught him hypnotized by her creamy thighs and hips.

"Excuse me, sir. What were you looking at?" She knew what he was looking at and was just spinning him, 'cause she caught him with his eyes full of her.

"Oh, nothing. My bad," Marty said.

"Quit being scary. You want my number?" she replied.

She wrote her number down. She could see the cause and effect that had taken place in his mind and placed him into the web that many had previously been caught in, only to be terribly disappointed. They never came close to the prize. On the slick, they called her Black Widow.

He grabbed the paper, then tried to spin off.

"I guess you don't want my name to go with that

number, huh? It's Sierra. Have a good night."

He quietly lay down in his *padrino*'s room and put his head on

the pillow, whispering, "Hurry up and get better so I can get you out of this living graveyard, old man." He smiled, and went to sleep and got plenty of rest.

Marty woke to the sun shining in his face. "Joy comes in the morning," he said, and opened his eyes to see the joy of his *padrino*'s eyes watching him.

"Yeah you right. Joy comes in the morning. You better be glad you didn't end up weeping last night after you called me 'old man'!" M&M said.

"Oh, *padrino*! You heard me?!"

"That's all I heard until you started snoring me out of my own room and things. I thought I was supposed to be the patient, but here you come, trying to steal my shine!" he exclaimed as his *ahijado* laughed.

Bad Boy was tickled to death by his *padrino*'s quick recovery—he had really heard him call him an old man!

"*Padrino*, you couldn't have been too sick if you heard all that," he said, tugging at his godfather.

"I was sick enough to hear you call me old! That was enough to send me to my maker!"

Doctor Motab walked in and heard them verbally

sparring back and forth.

"Mr. M, I see you're doing better, thanks to your godson. Your blood pressure is right where we want it to be. How are you feeling?"

"I'm ready to go home, M&M said.

"Your wish is my command. I'll have my nurse come in to assist you with the tests I need you to take before and after you eat. Write the numbers down for two weeks, then come in to see me at my office."

"Yes, sir! Thanks," M&M said.

"Don't thank me; thank your godson. He saved your life!" the doctor said, then left.

In came the nurse who had Bad Boy hypnotized, looking like she just stepped out of a *Chanel* magazine and into those scrubs.

"Hello, sir. I see you made it. Let me get your vitals here so you can be on your way. Sign those release papers, and we'll get you started."

The nurse began thoroughly doing her job, not paying attention to Bad Boy—not one iota. She finished up there, and Bad Boy stepped into the restroom, leaving his pills out. As she packed her patient's belongings, she stumbled upon Bad Boy's pills. At the same instant, Bad Boy was coming out of the bathroom when he noticed the nurse reading the bottles, then easing them into the bag with the tip of her fingers as if the bottles had poop on them.

Bad Boy backed up, closed and locked the door, and turned on the light. He flushed the toilet again and washed his hands. He grabbed a paper towel noisily, then walked out.

When he walked out of the bathroom, the nurse gave him that "ew" look, then reached in her pocket and pulled out a bottle of that antibacterial, no-rinse, no-wipe spray that's bound to kill any toxic bacteria. He caught on, and she gave him a smirk that said, "You dirty dippin', dude!"

Being so thrown off by her behavior, he walked out without his little Walgreens bag. He was trying to bounce and was halfway down the hall when Sierra said, "Mr. M&M! Excuse me, but your godson left his vitamins, knowing exactly what they were." She held the bag with the tips of two of her fingers. Marty walked back and snatched the bag out of her hand. He started to walk away when she said, "Better luck next time. What was your name, again?" Sierra said. Bad Boy never turned back around 'cause he was so embarrassed as his Nino watched them both following them with his eyes very much amused.

Love at first sight? M&M said jokingly

Bad Boy helped his *padrino* into the car and was heading home when his phone rang.

"Hello? ... *Padrino*, it's for you."

He passed his godfather the phone, and there was his

brother, coming to see him at the hospital.

M&M sang the lyrics of 50 Cent: "Go ahead and get your refund. I'm not dead!"

Then, he began laughing. "Come to *mi casa*!"

They pulled up to M&M's house. Bad Boy was gonna help his *padrino* out until he said, "¡Cuidado, mijo! Don't you see my girlfriend across the street watching? I don't want her to think your

padrino got no juice!"

"*Padrino*, I'm gonna return you to sender, 'cause you're not the same person!" He laughed.

"That's what the old lady gon' say when I get done with her. She gon' think I went and got Viagra!"

"Viagra?!!! Marty said laughing

Bad Boy used his own key and walked in, going straight to the kitchen and putting on some Folgers. He knew his *padrino* wanted or needed it. He might have even started to claim his sickness was from not having a cup of coffee a day, as he had all his life.

M&M had been very good to Marty all his life and was good to his mom, even going to the front of the line to get him back.

He had taken care of all the funeral arrangements—the burial, the clothes, everything. Marty loved his *padrino* for that.

Marty heard his *padrino*'s brother come in, but he went ahead and made M&M his favorite breakfast to go with the coffee.

Instead of grease, he used olive oil. His *madrina* always used to say, "Use olive oil to keep yourself healthy."

When he finished, he walked to the patio, where his *padrino* and *tío*, Ese's father, were sitting.

"¿No tienes hambre?"Marty asked if they were hungry. They said yes because they knew the only thing Marty knew how to cook was his *padrino* favorite breakfast, what he claimed to be the most important meal of the day.

They came, grabbed their plates and built them up, then grabbed some tortillas and chili.

Marty had made breakfast burritos filled with potatoes, eggs, meat and cheese. When M&M and Theo sat down, they dug right in. After Marty's *padrino* took the first bite and tasted that olive oil, he looked up at Marty, who laughed. M&M went to get his little diabetes case to check his blood sugar.

Taking that bite and tasting that olive oil stirred up his memory quick. He even heard his wife's voice telling him he had to eat better. He checked his sugar and realized he was a little bit low, so he ate real good to bring it up.

"Just like the doctor ordered," he said.

"Okay, *padrino*, I'm out! I have to go by the school to take a test," Bad Boy said

As Bad Boy was walking away, his godfather said, "Don't forget your vitamins, *mijo*, then laughed. Even though they didn't talk about those pills, M&M knew his godson was in good health, and the pills had to be only one thing.

Going on about his day, Marty was feeling better than he was yesterday. *So is my padrino*, he thought. He went to school to take the test, and Walah was there, doing the same.

"Man I was trying to reach you yesterday! You ready to go to Penn State's spring bling?"

"You know it!"

So, they tested, and began to talk about the exam after class.

"It's going down in Philly, yo! They gon' have surprise known rappers and all at the college!" Walah said.

"So, it's in two weeks, and we leave it on Friday at 2:45 p.m. You know my roommate going, so where should I make reservations at?" Bad Boy asked.

"Downtown Philly Sheraton on 13th and Filbert. That's where I'm booked. Call me and let me know, yo! Give them my name and tell them to give you the closest room possible to me," Walla said.

"I got you," Bad Boy said.

"Holla!" And Walah was gone, bumping Drake's "Marvin's Room" as he left.

Marty was hyped up about the trip until he looked over into the passenger seat, where his STD pills were. They reminded him how he was caught slipping when he was ridin' dirty that one time. That's all it takes—one time—for you to throw in the towel if you don't wrap that thing up.

People say an extra eight pounds will keep you off the team, and it will, but a baby is the least of all your problems if you catch something you can't get rid of! You feel me?

Marty had promised himself he would never go out like a sucker ever again. That girl could have had him lying on the cold slab. Lady Luck was on his side when he hit that three-in-one: gonorrhea, syphilis and chlamydia! *Yes, Marty,* he thought, *you're definitely a winner—or, better yet, a wiener.* He was out of pocket.

He headed to his apartment, where Ese was already in the lab, bagging and sagging and doing what hustler boys do.

"Ese, they can never call you a **** boy !" Bad Boy said.

"I bet you they know how to call me 'doughboy'! I got it better than Pillsbury."

The way he said Pillsbury had Bad Boy clamming up, 'cause he thought Ese was getting ready to go in on him. He soon realized that he wasn't, though; he was just trying to remember who was with the doughboy. Marty laughed and said, "I can dig it."

They started chopping it up about the college spring bling in Philly. They both agreed that they needed a vacation. Ese called and made reservations on the airline and at the Sheraton hotel on 13th and Filbert. Then, he called Enterprise to rent a Cadillac Escalade for the two weeks they planned to be there.

"Since we're gonna be gone for two weeks, I'm gonna work at the gym every day for the next three weeks and ask Tyriq if he wants to take time off," Marty said.

"Yo! Your boy or your boss man ain't going for that," Ese said.

"Yo! Stop playing with me, Ese," Bad Boy laughed..

"Don't trip, 'cause I'm gonna hold us down in this department," Ese said.

"Right, right," Marty said.

Bad Boy went to the restroom, took a shower and got ready for work, then headed out. He hit the E-way and got to work in a New York minute.

Pulling in, he saw the twins, Lil Lil and Big Big walking in with Great Grands. They were going into Sweet, Sexy and Sassy, so he headed that way.

Walking in, he said, "Hello, Miss Charlesetta! Lil Lil

and Big Big, come give your cousin a hug!" They did, and he told them both that he loved them.

"You, too," Lil Lil said.

"I love you, too, big cousin!" Big Big said.

He walked over and gave hugs to his aunt, Lil Mama, and Great Grands, who were heading to the casino to break 'em.

"Ain't seen you since in we were Casa Grande at your granddaddy's. How have you been, Miss Charlesetta?" Marty said.

"Yeah. My godfather almost died," she replied.

"What?!" Marty and Lil Mama both gasped.

"How come you didn't call nobody?" Lil Mama asked. Throughout the years, she got to know M&M, 'cause he always knew where his godson was.

"Auntie, he good, though. It was just diabetes," Marty said.

"Diabetes?!" Lil Mama exclaimed.

"I said the same thing! He at home, back to his ghetto self!" Marty laughed.

"Marty, how you gon' call that man ghetto when you more ghetto than him?"

Marty laughed, laughed then told them about his upcoming trip to Philly for spring break.

"You could stay at my house, son," Charlesetta said. She started taking the key off her key ring just that quick and gave it to him.

Marty didn't want to turn her down 'cause she was always so generous. Then, she wrote down the address.

"Thank you," Marty said as he programmed the address into his phone.

"Keep the key just in case you go, but you are more than welcome. That's the least I can do, since y'all won't ever let me do nothing else around here!" Miss Charlesetta said.

"Come on, Great Grands! I've been begging you to make that triple-layer German chocolate cake!" Bad Boy pressed.

"Well, son, it slipped my mind. "That's what happens when you get old," she said.

"Tell that to somebody else, Great Grands, 'cause your memory is better than an elephant's!

"Don't tell nobody that, son!" Miss Charlesetta laughed.

Marty headed to the gym. He found Tyrik in the office, going over the books, so he knocked on the door. Tyrik looked up, then waved him on in. Marty went in, closed the door and sat down.

"Tyrik, I apologize how I acted toward you the other day. And you was right; I was acting Joe. I changed the accounts back, so you can do what you gotta do. Thank you. You been good to me and my family. Thank you for letting people know that lives can change when love is in the equation. Thank you. For the next three weeks, you can take off if you want, and I got you," Marty said.

Looking at Marty and hearing his sincerity, he knew he wasn't being spent. "Marty, I'm gonna take you up on that."

Tyrik started laying his plan out and what he wanted to do. Marty found the plan to be solid, so he made a few plans and phone calls to cover the store for the next week,. He would need Ese's help, and Miss Charlesetta's, too.

Marty crept out the back door, then eased into the back entrance, where he knew he would find Miss Charlesetta before she headed out to the casino.

"Miss Charlesetta, can I walk you to your car? I need to speak with you." He then let her in on the plan.

"Sure. I'm down," she said.

He called M&M and asked him for accommodations. He, too, liked the idea, so he agreed. Everybody had the game plan down, so when Bad Boy got back to the gym, Tyrik headed out to handle his business. Hours later, he came in looking like the cat that swallowed the canary.

When Tyriq left, he went to the jewelers and bought a beautiful chain. He called and booked a suite for a week, then went and packed. When he came back, Marty went to add his two cents to the mix and hit game points.

The remainder of the day went by really smoothly; everyone was happy. Lil Mama was cleaning the store and making the money drop. Then, she locked the front door, set the alarm and had 60 seconds to get out the back door before she triggered the alarm. Doing that the last couple times had gotten on her very last nerve because the police had to come peep out the area and run her name. So, no, she was not going through that again.

She ran out the back door. She hated that the back light had died out 'cause the back of that building gave her the creeps, and she forgot to call the maintenance man.

She was fumbling in her purse for the keys that seemed to fall deeper into her purse, to the point she had to squat down, set her purse on the ground and hold the door shut to grab her key before locking the doors.

A second after she locked the door, two people grabbed her, and she tossed and turned in panic as they put tape over her mouth and a cloth over her eyes.

She exhausted herself to the point of losing consciousness.

Once the thugs got her where she was going, she awoke to the sound of someone rambling in her purse like they were looking for money or something. Inside of her mind, she hoped her pursuers would hurry up and find the large bills she had, so maybe they would let her go and not hurt her. All kinds of things went through her mind in this moment of devastation; she was tripping. Then, all of a sudden, someone came. *This has to be a strong man*, she thought as he picked her up and carried her somewhere, then put her in a car. It seemed to take a long time.

They rode for almost 30 minutes before the car stopped. The man picked her up again, then sat her on a bed and took the cloth off her head. She was afraid to open her eyes. After a couple minutes, curiosity killed the cat, so she opened one eye. She thought that the one eye was deceiving her, so she opened the other before she realized the tape was on her mouth. She began to scream, but of course, no one would or could hear her.

With the tape on her mouth, she felt silly, so she snatched it off. She couldn't even think straight as she started trying to choke the man, who couldn't do anything to get away 'cause she had superhuman strength.

"You son of a gun! I'm gonna kill you!" She continued to struggle until the dude started laughing.

"Okay, Lil Mama."

"Don't 'Okay, Lil Mama' me! Where we at, and why you scared the devil out of me?!"

"It was the only way I can get you to come with me..."

She had been kidnapped by Tyrik. She wanted to kill

him, but the surroundings didn't look familiar, so she couldn't leave until she figured out where they were. Then, she would leave him for good.

"Where we at?" Lil Mama asked.

From there, the scene began to unravel...

"Will you marry me?" On one knee, Tyriq placed the big, beautiful diamond that she had seen on Great Grands's hand on her finger.

"Let me find out Great Grands had something to do with this!" she said, half laughing.

"Please don't say another word, and allow me to put the cloth over your eyes once again..." Tyrik said, seductively enough to spark her interest and make her do as he requested.

"I already know I'm gonna regret this. Hurry! Come on!" Lil Mama said.

From there, Tyriq led Lil Mama to a place where there was a lot of noise, then led her to even more surprises. She wanted to tear that bandana off her head so she could see, but she didn't. Right when it got quiet again, Tyrik took off the bandana. They were in a room with rose petals everywhere; they emanated a delicious fragrance. She walked around the beautifully decorated room and found three bottles of white champagne, which she loved, being chilled inside a brass ice bucket, along with the finest china wine glasses. Opening up the closet to see if something was in there, she found her suitcases and two large boxes wrapped with Victoria's Secret silk with her name on them. She felt as if she was Cinderella. Then, someone knocked at the door.

Tyrik went to the door and opened it up. It appeared to be room service, who pushed in a beautifully decorated food service car with two covered meals and a beautiful white cake, designed with a photo of Tyrik and her.

The man and woman began setting the table and lighting candles. Then, the man and woman stood side by side. Tyrik grabbed her hand, and the ceremony began...

"Will you, Lil Mama, take this man to be your lawfully wedded husband; to have and to hold; to honor and to cherish from this day forward, in sickness and health, for richer, for poorer, till death do you part?"

After what seemed like an eternity, she said yes, then they all blew out air as if they had been holding their breath.

Then, Tyrik hurried and said, "I do! Before she changes her mind!"

"Boy, if you don't let him finish, I'll leave you right at this so-called altar!" Lil Mama turned to the officiant. "Wait a minute! Wait a minute. Are you really a preacher?!" Lil Mama asked.

"Yes, ma'am!" said the man.

"I just had to check your status to be sure," Lil Mama said. She had to say "Carry on," so the ceremony could resume. She had everybody on edge. *I know it serves them right, after all I had to go through*, she thought as she looked at the ring and spun it around her finger. She silently agreed to and expressed gratitude for it all, 'cause she knew that ring was Oprah status!

"At the moment, all she heard was, "I do."

Tyrik kissed her so good it rocked her world and bunched up her crunchies. After that, all she heard was the door close. Tyrik kissed her again, and it was lights out as she dropped it super low, lower than she ever had on Tyrik, leaving him restless and desperately wanting more.

Sherriff and Dulce took long walks on the beach and ate at the most romantic spots with the finest wines.

They were so into each other that if asked later, they would only vaguely remember what the restaurants looked like, let alone what was eaten. For their scrapbook, they had periodically each taken pictures of memorable moments for them to share with their children and grandchildren one day, if God so willed for them to live. Each day, every moment they spent together was like a puzzle of their love being created for today, tomorrow and forever. If there was a possibility to fall in love even more, they knew it was for themselves. All of Dulce's hopes and dreams had healed all that the devil stole from her. Each dude before had hurt her feelings because she was saving herself for a man who would patiently wait to honor her as the queen she was.

Her king now sat before her within her kingdom.

Naughty and Daisha were feeling as if one of God's angels had fell from heaven. Naughty was so happy; he wanted to scream because he couldn't believe that God had brought him from where he had been.

Looking at Daisha, he knew that God had lovingly and personally handpicked this beautiful woman to become his helpmeet. It was as if the rib of his very own was used in the creation of this wonderfully made woman.

Naughty gazed towards heaven and thanked the king of kings for this blessing. Seemingly responding to his thanks, a fallen star fell through the skies. He made a wish of God to bless every moment, every day, now until forever with overflowing cups of love, peace, joy, happiness, hope and health, as well as spirits pressed down and running over.

Naughty was in such a daze; he never heard Daisha say, "Naughty?"

Snapping out of his daze, he responded, "Yes, my love?"

"I love you so much."

"I love you, too." Then, he began kissing her passionately once again.

TJ and Teka were floating on clouds of love in each other's arms as they made love and whispered promises and silent vows among themselves. Looking into each other's eyes, they were able to see many tomorrows that held lots of pure happiness on a solid foundation of love.

TJ thought to himself:

This is the way love was intended to be. I would never do anything to lose this beautiful Black woman. She is my first thought when I wake up as well and my very last thought as I drift off to sleep.

Lying in this bed with her is what I've been missing all my life. A pure and true love will never fall, nor ever fade, as we anchor each other's hearts as a whole, binding the spirits and spiritually painting pictures of a love that is eternally happily ever after.

When Lil Mama woke up, at first she was puzzled as to where she was, but feeling that diamond and its heaviness, she remembered whose she was now.

She had previously told Tyrik no, always saying she wasn't ready. She really was, but she wanted him to be the man to step up to the plate—not just for himself, but for his whole future family. He did that!

She liked the feeling of someone other than herself taking control and not having to travel down the road of life alone. Things seemed so much brighter than they had ever been. It didn't feel like she was carrying a load that was too much for her.

She was overwhelmed, not in the sense of feeling like

she was drowning, but walking on sands of tranquility with the peace that passes all understanding. Feeling renewed in her spirit and rejuvenated within her soul by a love deeper than she had ever felt, she knew then that God had smiled down on her with His outstretched, almighty hand.

At the store, Great Grands was in high spirits. She wondered how Tyrik had pulled off that last part. She didn't agree with it, but she was sure that once he put that piece of rock on Lil Mama's finger, it would leave any woman—if not all women—an assurance of love, life plenty of laughter and the knowledge that everything would be all right.

She laughed to herself because she knew God had answered her prayer of her grandson sowing his wild oats and settling down with someone who would love him, bear his children and solidify his life in the Lord.

The twins didn't even know what was going on; they just knew their parents were gone. Great Grands wasn't going to spill them well cooked beans. She had been cooking them up in her kitchen from the moment she had heard about the twin girls. From the moment she first saw Big Girl, she had asked God to soften her heart, and let Him lead her to those grandbabies of hers.

Bless her heart, she thought. *Sad what happened to her.* But one thing she did know was that God had better plans for His glory.

Bad Boy and Ese had been holding the fort down. Tyrik wondered how they got Lil Mama to the plane without any problems, 'cause he wanted no part of that party, either. He knew that when Lil Mama was happy, everybody was happy. When she was mad, all hell always made it on earth in a vicious, evil way. So, he left that to them.

Marty had said he would take the blame; he wanted his aunty to be happily married.

He hadn't seen his sister in a while, and after texting her a few times to come kick it and getting no response, he just fell back. He knew his sister was growing up and becoming as beautiful as his mama, so she had her hands full. They had been well prepared for their spring break festival at Penn State. After they made reservations, he got to know Sapphire in a real way, and found that she was on his level and definitely on the same type of time he was on. She had all the makings of a ride-or-die chick, and he loved it! Sapphire had that Sapphire in her blood that kept your boy upgrading his game. Truth be told, based on what he could see lay beneath, she was 'bout that life. Maybe Cupid would score that thing for him...

Sapphire had hooked Ese up with her Puerto Rican mami, Jasmine, who had it like Jennifer Lopez. Jasmine was a virgin, too, which made Ese work harder —all jokes aside, he told Bad Boy he wanted to wife that. Because Bad Boy knew Ese, he wouldn't question his wish; once Ese made a decision, it was considered a done deal. That's how Ese got down.

Both were looking forward to spending time together. Ese had called and changed the reservations for a room once Jasmine was in the mix. When he told Bad Boy, he just smiled and gave him a pound.

Bad Boy also felt like he and Sapphire were compatible. Both their mothers had passed, so the loneliness thereafter was mutual. Both were raised by their grandmothers, so from there, they were definitely off to the races.

She had a brother who had run away to Florida to get away from his "gold-digging grandma," as he called her. Bad Boy had a sister he hadn't talked to in a minute. The more they talked, the stronger their connection got.

When Tyrik woke up, he had told Lil Mama he had a couple's massage set up, as well as pedicures and manicures, and she would be getting her nails and hair done by one of Marty's homegirls. So, Lil Mama ordered room service for breakfast.

While they waited, they made love, then took a shower. Their lovemaking was better than it had ever been, but she brushed it off as her no longer feeling guilty about having sex while not being married to her husband. Now, all those pressures no longer existed, and having another child or children with her husband didn't quite seem as far-fetched.

As they got out of the shower, there was a knock at the door, so Tyrik put on his housecoat provided by the hotel and went to the door. It was room service with their royal breakfast. Tyrik pushed the cart into the room, where Lil Mama had just put on her clothes. They sat down to eat, and Tyrik led them into prayer of thanks for the wholesome meal they had been given.

"Tyrik, just in case you're wondering... I'm so glad you made this happen the way you did. All my guards were let down, and I had no time to think of getting married. I only seen my life flashing before my eyes, wondering what could have been."

People in Da Grande kept calling Bad Boy, so he let them simmer. The longer he waited, the thirstier they became. He was planning on going late Thursday night, so the paper would really be stacked.

Since the numbers rang right in his head, he bounced out and was CG-bound like a bull in heat looking for a heifer.

Making it to the Casa Grande exit, it was all smooth sailing. Like a big dog, he eased on down the road like he was any character imaginable—except for ones who didn't have courage, of course.

He cruised from spot to spot, seeing that money dropping in his lap like he was making it rain! He was in a zone, cruising through the streets of CG—now you see your boy, now you don't ! He bumped his music as he turned down the "O," Westside Ocotillo, just sightseeing. Then, he headed down 10th Street. He saw Hollywood, D'Myron and Nate, his crew from back in the cut. Then, he saw the old booty call that had him hotter than an oven. Scoping her out, he decided he was goin' in for the kill... until he saw her lump of a stomach poking out. Seemingly, she wanted him to see it—and so did EVERYBODY else! It felt like his worst nightmare had come to reality, just when he was resurfacing in Casa Grande.

Again, the words he said previously came to mind: *Looking back was for suckers.*

Deep down inside, he had a feeling that it was his seed she was carrying.

He headed to his grandma's house, and his thoughts went in one ear and right out the other.

Walking in, he saw that she had made meatloaf, baked potato salad and Thousand Island dressing, with a big cup of Country Sweet mixed with grape and orange Kool-Aid, just the way he liked it.

"Hey, son! How are you? Come and give me a hug, and don't you bring that shit in here, either!" Luscious Bell said.

"That's what I won't be doing," Marty replied as he bit into the mouthwatering meatloaf.

He went into his mom's bedroom. He hadn't been in there in a minute. Big Girl's room was just as she had left it. When he laid down, her scent began to surround him, as she was embracing him. He had gone in there to talk to Sapphire and knew his grandma wouldn't come in there, but she would've, had he been in Lil Mama's room.

TMuch needed tears began to fall. The more they fell, the more relief he felt. He didn't know his grandma was at the door, crying and praying at the same time. She wanted come in and tell him everything would be all right. She knew he would've shut back up, just like he did when he had gone to his uncle's. Luscious Bell knew that in order for her grandson to survive, he needed to find his own way to healing. She had equipped him with the very tools to do so long ago; now, he had to want to survive. He required a desire, a hunger, to ease over the pain he had inside.

Luscious Bell wouldn't go to sleep because she wanted to be there if he needed her. To ease her own pain and worries, she began her spring cleaning. She shampooed the carpet in her room and washed the walls with Murphy Oil soap as she sang, "I love you; I need you to survive; you are important to me; I need you to survive."

Marty fell asleep as he heard his grandmother singing. Long ago, he slept with his mother, but now, he was older. She would tell him about how one day, he would be a father. She wanted him to be a father to his child, to give his child all that she had given him and more.

All of a sudden, he started dreaming. His mother had found his gun. They weren't at his grandmother's house, but at his own. She was crying, pointing at the gun she had found.

They began wrestling with the gun; she wanted to take it away from him 'cause she didn't want him hurting himself or anyone else. The gun went off. He heard her scream, just as he had when she died. She kept screaming and began pointing to his shirt. He became confused and the shining bright light above them began to darken. He looked at what his mom was pointing at, and instead of her being shot, he found himself shot...

Then, total darkness engulfed him.

Someone was knocking on his door. He jumped up, looked around, felt his chest and turned on the light—no blood. The person ws knocking harder. He opened it up and his grandma was standing there.

"Son, come into the living room for a minute. We need to talk!" Luscious Bell said.

The tone of her voice was so stern that he knew not to question her. She was still the head of the house and of his life. He also knew that disobedience would not ever be put up with, so he just went with the flow.

Heading down that long hallway seemed even longer than usual because of the fire that was coming out of his grandma's ears. He knew he was the cause of her anger; he just didn't know what he did. As the long hallway began to end and opened into the living room, he saw the problem, the cause of the fire. He knew that surely, this was smoke that even a fire extinguisher couldn't put out. All he could do was sit down; what else could he do, run?!

"First of all, it seems like I spoke the devil into existence, doesn't it?" She smiled, and he shook his head in agreement.

Right when he felt like he made it safely out of the field of landmines, one exploded.

"Son! Can you tell me about this?" Luscious Bell shouted, pointing towards the girl.

He tried to play crazy. "What?"

"Marty Lemons!" she roared.

"I'm sorry, Grandma!" Looking at the girl, he said, "Since you here, say what you gotta say!"

Like his grandma, he took the powerful and authoritative role, saying those words with a harshness so sharp they could have cut cheese with the lightest pressure.

Alissa tried to stand her ground. "You know what we did in that back room at the end of the hallway!"

Luscious Bell leaned in a little to scare the girl. "Baby, why don't you tell me what you did in MY"—she emphasized her words—"back room, since it was MY back room?"

Luscious Bell knew exactly what happened, exactly with whom, in exactly which room.

"Well?" Luscious Bell said, waiting.

"I'm pregnant by you!" Alissa said.

"You hope! Or, it could be the same dude that gave you the STDs! Yes, more than one *or* two—three!" Marty said, going straight for the jugular. He knew this would blow her socks off in embarrassment!

The sting of his words stunned her, so she jumped up and ran out the door as his laugh echoed to the core of her soul.

As the girl tore out of there like a bat out of hell, Luscious Bell was still in the same uproar she had originally been in. She was still sitting on the couch with the same look, but more petrified now. She silently demanded and awaited an explanation. If he played as crazy as he had earlier, she was ready to go AWOL upside his head, 'cause no one, absolutely no one, would assassinate her character or question her integrity! NO ONE!

After Luscious Bell locked the door behind her, Marty was giggling—until he saw the look on his grandma's face. Her expression said, "Let's get down to the nitty-gritty!"

"Grandma, I'm not sure if the child is mine. If it is proven, then I'm willing to act accordingly. Now, about the three-in-one: She hit me with her burner and gave me chlamydia, gonorrhea and syphilis. All of it has long been cured as she was cast back into the fire she sent my way! That was the first and the last time I'll get caught slipping, so don't worry. I remember what you told me long ago, and I won't bring no hussies here," Marty explained.

"Now that you've done said what needed to be said to me, I'm satisfied," Luscious Bell said.

"Granny was ready to go in on her, huh?" Marty laughed.

"You, too, if you hadn't cowered down! She had nerve, darkening my doorstep like I owed that heifer anything! God, forgive my sass," Luscious Bell said.

"Don't trip. We got this," Bad Boy said.

"Have you seen Lil Mama? I've been calling her and getting no answer. I even called the store to leave a message," Luscious Bell asked.

"You don't know?!" Bad Boy gasped. "Tyrik took her to elope, but we got the kids and everything. They supposed to be back tomorrow."

"Hush your mouth, grandson!" Luscious Bell was tickled on that note, 'cause she knew her daughter was fighting her tooth and nail 'bout hers. "Bless their hearts. I hope she do it..."

Bad Boy started telling his grandma how it all went down, and she almost looked like a rattlesnake that was welled up and ready to strike.

Tyrik an Lil Mama had really been relaxing, as they

would treat each other to massages each had learned from the masseuses. They had both emotionally and spiritually taken things to another level and were filling each other's souls.

Tyrik had begun to lose hope in trying to lead his now-wife to the water, desiring her to drink from a well that was going dry.

When Marty had that power trip and messed with the accounts, in all actuality, that had been the straw that broke the camel's back. Had Marty not apologized as Tyrik was going over the books to check any errors that may have slipped his mind, he definitely would have been ready to throw in the towel.

All was said and done. Everyone was more on the same track, heading in the right direction for the good of the whole, not just for oneself. Iron sharpens iron when working together.

So much water has passed under the bridge for the whole family, Lil Mama thought. The acts of love from not just Tyrik, but from all who loved her enough to work together for the family, created the essentials to bring hope and balance into her life. This love opened doors for her and enabled her to broaden her horizons and make right what many thought to be wrong.

Lil Mama thought to herself, feeling blessed, for her road in life could have been unkind and treacherous, just as her sister's had been. Looking back, Lil Mama remembered the time when she had been angry with her mother for spending more time with Big Girl, even to the point of being jealous. Instead of being jealous, she could have been loving, even more so as she took her sister's time in the land of the living for granted.

When Lil Mama had gotten pregnant, Big Girl was the sister she has always been: a shoulder to cry on, loving when she felt unloved, and hopeful when she felt hopeless. Big Girl had taught her how to soar as an eagle, high into the skies.

Big Girl gave her the foresight that she wasn't a chicken who she hung around, but an eagle who soared high, recreating herself each year to fly even higher.

Tyrik and Lil Mama had found that courting each other and having quality time didn't end once they got married. They continued doing all the things they did in the beginning. They talked as adults, and Lil Mama kept herself up as a lady, getting her hair and nails done and looking pretty, as a woman should. She recreated herself regularly to be every woman her husband would need; this kept him focused and balanced.

Tyrik wanted to keep chivalry alive in their marriage. He complimented his wife, helped her and remained attentive to her every need. Every man knows that if Mama ain't happy, he won't be, either!

Every day being married should remain as sweet as the very first day that had you broken your neck to see. You must reroute your path to get each other's attention as you had in the beginning.

Marriage is not the end, but truly the beginning of love. It seals and solidifies each other's very soul, just as intended.

This would be the last day of their honeymoon, but the first day of a path created in love for man, woman and children to work together. As iron sharpens iron, they solidify a foundation to remain balanced on the rock of salvation, anchored and grounded with roots deep within the soul of the plentiful harvest.

No matter what storms may come their way, they knew that whatever brought them together would keep them together. As love conquers all, it heals and restores the mind, body and soul, spiritually and emotionally, in all the most essential ways.

Love is also communication. This brings understanding, which leads to unconditional love. Life won't always be a bowl of cherries or strawberries, so take what ingredients you are able to use and add them to the fruits of the spirit. Always go the extra mile for the one you love in the beginning; do not wait until the end of each day or the end of your lives. Many have either lost or given up on love, or even taken it for granted. *Always remember*, thought Lil Mama, *that God is love. How could I ever give up on Him?*

Not taking a moment away from each other, Tyrik and

Lil momma made love in its wholeness for hours on end. They ordered room service, drinking everything from wine with cheese and crackers to full-course meals. As there time began to wind down to hours, the minutes they had together was spent cherishing the love they had found in each other. This love ignited the fire within their souls that complemented each other entirely. When they boarded the plane, it was as if each step brought blessings of love that propelled them forward into a life eternal, in each other, through God here on earth. They looked through the clouds and felt like eagles, having the ability to soar not just through the clouds of love, but through life's clouds that wouldn't rob them of the harvest that they would continue to cultivate as one.

Living life together as a whole was new and interesting in every aspect.

M&M's private plane was utilized to the fullest capacity as they made love, hugging, kissing and touching as if it was their very first time.

Their touchdown at the municipal airport came way too soon. Walking out of the plane felt precious and promising. Even the atmosphere was impressive to accommodate the lovebirds. Holding hands, they headed to their car that remained parked where it was left.

"Don't think I forgot about how you kidnapped me! If our love wasn't as good as it was, I would call the popo on you! But since we both got that 'actright,' I'll find other ways to violate you in the names of love, putting shackles on your heart—and on that package in them briefs," Lil' Mama said.

"Sounds good to me! I guess I'll take all the credit now," Tyrik said.

"What you mean?" Lil Mama asked.

"If you had been mad, I would have blamed it on my co-conspirators!" They both laughed.

When they made it home, the girls were out of school and Great Grands was in the kitchen cooking chicken and dumplings. She had the whole house's mouths watering and tongues a-waggin'.

"Grandma, I love and appreciate you so much," Tyrik said, giving her love.

"Oh, you made it back?" Charlesetta was surprised and happy.

"Yeah, we made it back!" Lil Mama walked in, crying and thanking Great Grands.

"So, it went all right? Amen! Now, you know I ain't told my grandbabies, 'cause I didn't know if you would kill my grandson or call the police! I wasn't saying nothing, so you might as well call them in here and tell them, 'cause I want to see them faces of mine," Great Grands said.

"Lil Lil!" their daddy called.

"Big Big!" Lil Mama called.

Before they knew it, they heard little feet beating the ground, screams and tears of joy from them all as Lil Mama showed the girls the diamond. They looked at their grandma's hand; she smiled, hid her hands behind her back, took off one of her rings and placed it on her bare ring finger.

Tyrik said, "We's a-married now, chillen!" like Oprah Winfrey in *The Color Purple*.

Then came more screams as Great Grands

pulled the peach cobbler from the oven. She told the twins to set the table.

"You two," she pointed at Tyrik and Lil Mama, "have a seat while your daughters serve their parents. See you young'uns later. I'm going to the casino!" Great Grands hugged and kissed them all on her way out.

The girls set the table as Great Grands had taught them while their parents were gone, serving the food on the plates, wonderfully proportioning it as if it were a work of art.

They placed the plates in front of their parents, made their own and then sat down across from each other as their parents sat at each end of the table. Right when Tyrik was getting ready to lead in prayer, Big and Lil began:

"Before the throne of grace and mercy, humbly and in reverence of our Heavenly Father, we give thanks for all that You have blessed us with. Thank You for giving us all a mind to want to serve You and no other. Thank You for blessing our parents' union, as well as the union of the body as a whole, in the kingdom of our royal family here on earth, where we serve a living God who is no longer on the cross, but in the land of the living. Thank You for placing a hedge of protection around us, covering us with your blood. In Your precious son's name we pray, amen."

"Amen! That was a blessing! Thank you both so much," Lil Mama said.

"Yes! Thank you, Daddy's beautiful little girls," Tyrik agreed.

"Now, can we get our grub on before it gets cold?!" Lil Lil asked.

"Ya mean!" Big Big said, all hip.

"Ride out, soldiers!" Tyrik shouted.

"Knock knock!" Bad Boy called out as he and Ese came in.

"Hello! Glad you made it back safe!" Ese said.

"Bad Boy and Ese, come give y'all auntie a hug!" Lil Mama said.

The softened gangsters headed over to her. She jumped up and grabbed both of them by their necks, holding on and trying to choke them as they laughed, parading her around the living room.

"Is that how you feel, Auntie?" Bad Boy asked jokingly.

"No, Mama. What I want to know is, how you jumped all the way on them dudes?!" Tyrik intervened, laughing.

"By thinking about how these crooks helped you!"

"Helped do what?" Bad Boy asked.

"Don't play crazy—neither one of you crooks!" Lil Mama said, laughing.

"Well, we headin' out to our spring bling!" Bad Boy said.

"Be careful! And call us when y'all get there! Too bad y'all aren't going by force, huh?" Lil Mama joked.

"C'mon, now. You benefitted with that big ol' Rock of Gibraltar on your finger!" Ese said.

"Let's go," Bad Boy urged.

As they all laughed, Big Big cleared her throat to bring their attention back to eating. She was so loud that they all started laughing again.

"Does that mean you're hungry, Mama?" Tyrik asked Big Big.

"You know that's right!" She went straight in on that plate—there was no misunderstanding that she was hungry!

As a family, they finished eating. When they were all done, the girls cleared the table and cut each family member a big piece of cobbler.

When everyone finished their dessert, the twins excused

their parents, informing them they would be clearing the table, washing the dishes and cleaning up before they got their baths. Their homework was all done.

"Thank you! Can we each get a hug and kiss, little ladies?" their mother asked through tears, knowing that her daughters were definitely growing into little ladies.

TJ and Teka made it back from the place for lovebirds, touching down at the airport in Phoenix feeling relaxed, with sound, peaceful minds. They headed to the shuttle that they had arranged to head back to Casa Grande, where they would reside in unity. Upon their return, Teka would attend Central Arizona College in the outskirts of Casa Grande. She would then major in accounting and business management. This would allow her a position at Wells Fargo Bank, where Lety had arranged for her, Daisha and Dulce to work in different areas within the bank.

TJ would still be at Empire Personal Delivery Service, Inc., as secondary executive officer to Naughty, who would manage all the business under their incorporated umbrella.

They headed on home because come that Monday morning, they would then pursue their lives, together, as a family. Teka and TJ were both planning to be pregnant.

Sherriff and Dulce almost missed their plane homebound 'cause they couldn't get enough of each other. They almost made love in the limo on their way to the airport—had the driver not put the divider down, they would have. They guessed he had to be eavesdropping. So, they just opted to sip from the chilled crystal glassware that was complimentary with the limo service; apparently, so was his nosiness.

All in fun, feeling well loved and happily married, Sherriff had hopes of expanding the cell phone service business, proposing to purchase a building to lease to their incorporation.

Dulce would also be attending school at Central Arizona college with the other two girls, and would be working at the bank as well. Dulce also had a desire to open a daycare business for kids as a part-time job. Sherriff, on the other hand, was ready to practice filling up their house with kids. He told his wife he wanted eight, and she responded, "Is that all?"

Naughty and Asia sat in first class, sipping on some Dom Pérignon and eating caviar, feeling at ease and accomplished together as they looked out into the skies. Their minds raced:

Being on the bottom so long, your boy was bound to come up, you heard! Here I am, in the big bird in the sky, chilling with wifey. Oh, how good it feels to be with the woman who I love, married to her and heading home to our nest of love, Naughty thought.

Ain't nothing better than sitting next to this thorough

dude, who is my husband. God couldn't have chosen a better angel to allow Cupid to sort his arrow of love, hitting the bullseye on the heart of hearts. God has definitely sent me an angel to love, honor and hold as together we explore the deepest of love, Asia thought to herself.

Touching down on the east coast, Bad Boy, Ese and Walah were at Philadelphia International Airport. The three had never seen so many Blacks together in one place—where smiles were everywhere, no fighting, no arguing. They were amazed.

They caught the cab to north Philly, to the Sheraton Hotel, where they would reside for the next two weeks in and around sheer elegance to let a brother know it really could be done.

Ese, was born and raised in Las Cruces, New Mexico by his father, Juan D. and mother, Alice D. They moved Arizona to build a better life for themselves and their family. Mrs. D worked at the hospital, and Mr. D worked odd jobs out and about.

Growing up and being friends with Ese had its benefits of a cool, fun and crazy big family that worked together with what they had. A lot of times, all they had was each other, but that was enough for them. Bad Boy considered himself blessed to be amongst their family; there was never a dull moment. This is where he picked up Spanish.

He remembered that way back when, Mrs. Alice D told him that in order to eat at her table, he had to learn Spanish. He ate a lot at their table and learned a grip of Spanish that helped him throughout life—not just in the dope game, but in real life.

Walah was just easing in the cut, watching these two dudes look around like they were in Hollywood amongst the stars. Bad Boy was a star! For real, for real. You heard?!

Bad Boy was feeling proud of his city. This was where Arizona met Philly; where Hershey's chocolate kept them all covered in dark chocolate, brown skin, light skin. Yes to chocolate! Here, they were on the right type of time.

Like witnessing magic, they had to step outside of the block and see what was really hitting outside, on the other side of that block... You know, broaden their horizons and things. Doing so allowed them to acquaint themselves with others.

Ese put Bad Boy onto the most beautiful trees that were wonderfully cropped year-round in full harvest.

This happened because of Arizona's awesome sunny skies and soils of the richest fields that were famous for their cotton and the fruits of the land. Yes, indeed...

Many have said separation makes the heart grow fonder...

Looking around Philly and being away from home, Bad Boy concurred with the best of them. But he was still gonna stay west of them, you heard? 'Cause Pennsylvania got a wheel of its own, and it taught your boy a thing or two. From here, they say the grass is greener on the other side, and that's for a real reason and season.

"So, fellas, what's good to you?" Walah asked. "Yooooo! I'm feeling this!" Bad Boy replied.

"Me, too! It's greater later with my Puerto Rican mami, you heard!" Ese said.

Pulling up at the Sheraton in Center City with ghetto superstar clothing everywhere in sight, the gang began looking around. You'd swear Sassam Hussein's relatives were everywhere, but they were cool. After talking to them, Bad Boy thought, *They blacker than me! They said I'm white compared to them. They know more about hog mount, chitlins and rooter to the tooter than me. I'm like, "Wait a minute! Ain't you Muslim and don't eat pork?"*

The Native American guy told Bad Boy, "Brother, you got it twisted!" And he laughed till he cried when he said it in his Middle Eastern accent.

Walah called his girl. Bad Boy and Ese informed Sapphire and Jasmine that they were all in Philly. They made plans to eat at Miss Tootsie's soul food joint.

Real soul food was served at Miss Tootsie's! At first, they thought, *Seeing is* believing—but tasting is finger-, fork- and plate-licking good! Each of the fellas was nervous in their own way about meeting up with the honeys, then going to spring fling together. It was going to be a sight to see.

Bad Boy called his family to let them know he was good, so they didn't worry. He wanted to call M&M, but he knew that he would send an all-points bulletin to his mob partners, who would protect him worse than a mother hen.

Bad Boy didn't mention his whereabouts; he just said, "I'm cool" when asked. In response, they said, "Good."

With the first day planned, family members called when it was time to head to King of Prussia to get some G-wear.

Walking into King of Prussia Mall and heading to Foot Locker, these young bucks was like kids in a candy store with all the varieties of shoes the east coast carried as opposed to the west coast.

Bad Boy and Ese were shoe freaks, so they ordered varieties for them, M&M and Ese's Pops and had them all mailed to M&M's house. They grabbed two pairs off the racks to sport while in Philly. Wallah, wasn't too enthused, but he still bought two pairs of kicks there.

From there, they headed to Neiman Marcus and got the east coast's up-to-date attire of the latest fashions and underclothes.

Walking right out of Neiman Marcus, they saw a Gucci retail store, so they bought hats, watches, shoes, short sets and swimsuits for them and their girls, with swim shoes to match.

They bought outfits of different kinds and mailed them home to M&M—of course, lacing the godfather in the process. He did lace them

with some stacks. They then went into Louis Vuitton and did the same. The things they bought there had dope money written all over it. After spending all that money, they were hungry and thirsty, so off they headed to Master Wopp's Chinese jawn. That had da boys feeling fat in their pockets and their guts!

On the cab ride back to the Sheraton, they saw the Liberty Bell on Independent Avenue and the art museum they would be taking their girls to the next day. Feeling sleepy, they went on upstairs to rest for the next few hours before they were to meet the ladies at Miss Tootsie's for dinner. Then, they would be going to the movies at The Pearl.

Once these things were done, they planned on going back to the hotel, where the ladies would all spend the night with their fellas. Prior to that, they discussed the potential awkwardness; they all agreed they were comfortable with each other and had no problem with this being their first time meeting in person.

The Sheraton front desk clerk gave each room a wake-up call, letting them know they had now a driver whom would accommodated them, since they were of VIP status—well, M&M was. Thanks to M&M, they had benefits of every kind that they planned to utilize. They got dressed and headed downstairs to the car and driver, each feeling refreshed and chatty. They headed on to the restaurant, where, to their surprise, the ladies were already there. They were seated in a well-picked, secluded area that the six of them could enjoy. Because they were underage, there would be no consuming specialty beverages of any kind, unless "virgin" preceded the name. When the trio walked in, Walah's girlfriend, Jennifer, ran to him and jumped into his arms, hugging and kissing him. Sapphire shyly embraced Bad Boy, who picked her up and kissed her, spinning her around in his arms. Sapphire had on a casual Chanel outfit, with the cutest low-heeled sandals that looked like Cinderella owned them. Jasmine walked over and gave Ese a kiss. For more cause-and-effect, he grabbed her hand and kissed it. She was wearing a Jennifer Lopez-style two-piece Spanish body wrap, nipped and tucked in all the right places, with some Donna Karan high-heeled sandals fit for a goddess!

"So, gents how was your trip, might I ask?" Jennifer began.

"Very interesting, my love," replied Walah.

"Very relaxing," Bad Boy said.

"The anticipation of meeting you all was very unbearable for me," Ese said, looking into Jasmine's eyes.

Immediately, they both felt the butterflies, mixing up their words with all the anxieties of making this first impression count. Bad Boy and Sapphire had a current between them that was unseen to others, yet undescribable even to each other—they would later say this when asked.

Dinner went without incident, as the anxieties of "boy meets girl" disappeared. For dinner, they ate barbecued state, shrimp, lobster, potato salad and red velvet cake.

The movie was scheduled to start in 30 minutes, so they headed on over to The Pearl to see the latest *Transformers* movie. The line was very long, but when they got inside, they were able to find good spots. As the movie began, the fellas went to get popcorn, red vine licorice, Butterfingers, Snickers and chips to make sure they had it all, but they eventually had to go back to the concessions stand for drinks. The couples got cozy and close, exchanging pecks of kisses and tongue teases. When the movie was over, none of them could tell you what the movie was about. They could tell you they had a good time, though!

They still had a few candy bars, which the girls just put in their purses.

The driver showed up right on time as they went back to their hotel rooms, where they all began to relax.

They watched movies late into the night. Half-asleep, half-awake, Jennifer and Walla made love all through the night, trying to make up for months past and maybe a little bit for the future too. As the sun was coming up, they both fell asleep.

Ese was a gentleman all through the night—until Jasmine said, "Papi, I want all of you."

"Are you sure? Because I want you, too."

"But—"

"Now and forever, girl!" "Don't play, Ese! Let's see how my first time goes," Jasmine said.

Ese was even more nervous than she was, until they begin kissing passionately. He kissed her from head to toe over and over again, awakening her every being until she couldn't take it anymore.

"*Papi, estoy lista*," Jasmine said, meaning that she was ready.

Ese reached inside his wallet and pulled out a condom. Jasmine grabbed it, threw it in the trash and said, "Let fate decide for us if you're really serious about now and forever, but I'm gonna finish school. "

"¿En serio?" Ese asked.

"I can show you better than I can tell you," Jasmine said as she began kissing him in all the places that he had kissed her to drive her to this point of no return.

Every kiss became more seductive than the first, then erotic, to the point Ese felt he was going to lose his mind.

He was still bouncing, trying to get his mind right, as he

didn't want to get caught slipping like Bad Boy did.

I'm not Bad Boy! he thought. From there, he began to wonder where that came from. He took the control back from Jasmine, then began sending her spinning back to the web she had just begun to cast with him. Then, he went in gently, with kisses like those of butterflies.

Jasmine knew he couldn't believe how she was ready to get down, so she had to take him there, 'cause she wasn't leaving there a virgin. She didn't want to miss out on what she felt was the chance of a lifetime of love; an opportunity like this only came few and far between, if not at all. She knew when Ese's top begin to spin, as he started the love bites... Oh, pain for a few seconds, then pleasure. Two tidal waves of actright had come over her, leaving her feeling even more in love.

Ese felt like he done went made it rain silver and gold coins everywhere. He knew in his mind he wouldn't second-guess this decision that he had made as a man.

Growing up, he had always been responsible as the youngest boy. Plus, he had to look out for his baby sister, Pebbles.

He didn't know how he was gonna close that gap of many miles, but he knew he would. Jasmine was already a senior in high school, so a few months from now, she would graduate.

Jasmine started working when she was 15, and she would be turning 18 in a month, so she already saved a couple of dollars to head for the hills. Her body was like, *wow!* So, being tired of the advances of her uncles and cousins trying to pimp her out, she knew when the time was right, she would bounce.

For the last couple weeks, her TaTa was looking a little thirsty towards her, which let her know the time was coming closer. At the time, though, she was good, 'cause her Nana was always peeping things like that ever since she got hit on by her cousin when she was 14.

Jasmine knew that she was on borrowed time in the matter. Hitting paydirt with love, she saw the opportunity that she had been waiting for. She also knew that Ese was a solid dude on the right type of time, heading in the right direction with dreams of found love, life and balance.

They made love all through the night, climbing mountains of passion together and finding rocks to build on. Ese could see the rocks that she had collected in her life up to this point were chipped, shattered or broken, but that didn't bother him because he knew love could heal, seal, kill or steal depending on the method of madness, the person giving this love and their intent.

In all the lovemaking, he knew his heart. Knowing himself and his intent, he knew that his love would heal and seal the pieces of her life that had somehow become shattered.

As the sun began to peek through the low clouds and rise into the sky somewhere, some way, somehow, they drifted into togetherness on solid grounds of safe harbors.

Next door wouldn't have a clue that storms of love, peace, joy and passion had built a wall around them to protect the decisions they made together. Ese didn't want to have unprotected sex 'cause he didn't know her like that, nor did he want to chance ruining the gem that he now had. They watched movies, played video games and had serious talks about their families and how their mothers died.

10:00 a.m., Sheraton Hotel

They all awakened to wake-up calls from room service, telling them they would have breakfast delivered and they had an hour until their drivers would show up for their day of all sightseeing.

Walah and his girl got out of bed and took a shower, then began to eat their pork-free diet, as they were Muslim. Being raised on pork, at times, he felt rebellious. When he was in Arizona, he was trying to eat whole pigs and things! In the city, he lived by the phrase, "Alhamdulillah," meaning "All praise be to God," and practiced salat daily. It even looked like he had the spot on his forehead darkened.

Truth is, when he left the city, he began using Fashion Fair concealer over the spot so he didn't have to be bothered about his service to Allah. What a fraud, right? Ha!

Even though he was committing spiritual fraud, he still had a really good time with this girl, Jennifer, who he loved and would soon marry. They were both saving money for her to move out to Arizona.

Bad Boy and Sapphire took their respective showers, then got dressed to go out. No sooner than their forks hit their plates, they were challenging each other in another game, laughing and having a good time all over again.

"Oh! I got something for you," Bad Boy said.

"For me?!" Sapphire asked, surprised.

"Who else in this peace, Shorty? Of course it's for you!"

He went to get the surprise from the restroom. She had seen it peeking out of the bag earlier—curiosity killed the cat. She eased it on out of the bag, thinking it was his girlfriend's and he was trying to play her.

All that slipped her mind the moment he said he had something for her. So, when he came out with a few of the hottest pieces in exactly her size, 'cause he got her size from Jasmine, she was looking stupid sick!

"What's wrong? You don't like it?"

Bad Boy was about to trip until she said, "SIKE! Thank you! I love them."

"Not enough to try them on?"

The phone rang, interrupting their moment.

The front desk was calling; the driver was waiting.

Bad Boy was saved by that phone call. Sapphire had her "I have an attitude" face on; he wanted to get the situation right!

One thing Bad Boy couldn't stand was somebody who was unappreciative or a complainer.

If a woman wanted him to walk, all they had to do was exhibit either trait—that's a wrap!

They all walked into the hallway to meet as they headed to see the sights together, eyeing one another and wondering, *Did you hit? Did you smash? Did you pump?*

None of these questions were going to be answered anytime soon 'cause they were staying the weekend.

Feeling refreshed, everybody was in high spirits as they got into their car. They headed over to the Liberty Bell, then to the art museum and around Center City, shopping and just enjoying each other as they bought different things for different family members.

At 12:00 noon, they began to get hungry. There was a variety of food carts to choose from all around downtown Philly.

Everyone opted for Mexican hot dogs that were charbroiled right in front of them, then placed on a bun with jalapenos, salsa or what have you! They were served with tater tots and soda on the side.

Sitting down in a clean area under the trees, they had a picnic. As they finished eating, they headed to the Philly Zoo, where they saw all kinds of exotic birds and animals they hadn't seen before. Then, they headed into the arena, where they touched dolphins and took pictures.

All in all, they had a wonderful day. The fellas bought the ladies things that they liked as souvenirs.

Ese bought Jasmine a beautiful tennis bracelet and a ring with pearls, emeralds and a diamond in the center that sat up high.

Bad Boy said to himself, *This dude hit to be making it rain like this!*

Ese had seen his reaction, but was unfazed by what his homie thought. *Get lost.* He had mad respect for him, not to the point of second guessing himself, let alone sacrificing his happiness for him or anyone else.

All was well at the end of the day; each of their hearts was content.

With the sun going down, their driver reappeared. They all got in and headed back to the hotel to enjoy Netflix and have dinner be delivered by room service.

Having their own rooms gave them all time to enjoy themselves. They were at total ease as they lounged in the presence of all things hoped.

Jasmine had been feeling like a princess ever since he

copped that rock for her with the matching tennis bracelet.

She knew she had made the right decision, and never looked back on it.

Having made up his mind, he got his mind right. He had googled a justice of the peace, who was able to come through. He wanted to call her bluff if there was one.

Quiet as it was kept, none the wiser, they got married. Jasmine was even happier because she didn't want to accept no wooden nickels, as she had rolled the dice and won herself love and freedom.

Casting all cares to the wind, they made love as if they were dying soon. They spoke of things she dreamed and hoped for since she was a little girl.

Jasmine's mother was a heroin addict who supported herself using the fruit of the streets. They had an apartment in the projects for years until the measly $60 was too much of a hassle for her mom to sacrifice getting high as opposed to getting kicked out of her home. What really sealed the deal of getting her kicked out was that she let her light bill get three months past due. Her water, which is the cheapest utility in the nation by far, got cut off.

From there, Child Protective Services were called, and so were Jasmine's grandparents.

Even though Jasmine had close calls with her cousins and uncles, she had even closer calls due to her mom's negligence. She would wake up many nights with different dudes rubbing on her, leading her to screaming so loud everybody on her apartment floor was alerted. After a few times, the Black lady next door caught on and came to save her, finding her mother wasn't there. She had told Jasmine to grab a few things; she would stay with her until her mother came back.

When she did return, the lady stood at the door. She told Jasmine's mother, "I ought to whip your tail for this stunt. You trying to push your tricks off on your daughter 'cause your tail so dirty that not even the most desperate men want it! Let me hear that gal scream again, I'll be right over there shooting off that doorknob and hoping it hits you so I don't have to beat you to death!"

Jasmine had been standing right there, listening as she ate a good meal from the woman next door. Her mama had "forgotten" to feed her in the name of those 100 cc she wanted to put in her veins instead.

When Jasmine saw her mom, she was gonna head on out, 'cause she didn't want no smoke. Her mama hated when people were all up in her Kool-Aid when they didn't know the flavor! Apparently, this lady did know the flavor. She told Jasmine to finish her food and slammed the door. She became a friend and protector to Jasmine.

Her name was Rosalina, and her friend, Miss Lisa, worked to aid those who were less fortunate, had hit rock bottom and were ready and willing to be helped in the most essential ways to their survival. These ladies had inspired Jasmine to maintain her self-respect, which was based on morality. Because of these women, when times got tough, and the bulls in heat nipped at her heels, she had a place to run to that was filled with hope and love. Rosalina and Miss Lisa took the time out of their lives and checked in on her once a week, one on Friday and the other on Monday.

Jasmine thought to herself:

The simplicity of just caring enough for a person to spend your time and love to invest in them is, and always will be, treasured as better than any silver, gold or promissory note.

How I know this to be true is because these women believed in me, helping me to stand upon a solid foundation. As I am in the midst of my own storm, I know that I can make it with the help of these ladies. They took their time out for me and will lead me to my greatest success in life to live dreams I once thought far-fetched.

Jasmine thought about these very things Jasmine all through the night when she and Ese weren't making love. She knew that her ship had finally made it in, as she would be able to step out in strength and faith into a world that she could share with none other than her husband and children.

She wouldn't forget her abilities to make it through

danger and treacherous waters; after all, making it this far, she knew that her Maker had placed the heads of protection all around her when He heard her cries of fear.

Hearing about her older cousins who had been abused throughout their families and looking at many of their lives in the present moment, she was able to attest that each was still experiencing mental trauma. Because of such things in the past, she was able to hopscotch right over to safe ground.

Knowing or not knowing the eyes or thoughts of other people, she knew that days and times were troubled. So, she would keep an ever-watchful eye out as those ladies did for her. She wanted no one else to have to endure the curse she did.

Although many have lost their lives trying to survive the internal wounds of being molested by throwing in the towel, I haven't strength to fight, nor do I even want the strength to survive.

Slowly but surely, I'm learning that the battle that I fight today doesn't belong to me, but to the Lord for His glory. I will continue to fight the good fight of faith that I have heard of.

Every day, as I was the weakest, I am getting stronger and stronger... I am making it, and so can you. Just stand up.

Walah and Jennifer we're doing their income taxes in hopes of reaping a nice piece back to put a down payment on their house in Arizona. They enjoyed playing Yahtzee, backgammon, chess and checkers together. They didn't like Monopoly; the money part was discouraging to them.

Walah and Jennifer were together since they were 13. Long ago, 10 years later, they loved each other even more.

The plans they had made long ago were beginning to come to fruition in their careers as well as their lives. They agreed upon having four children: two when they first got married, and two, God willing, after their 10th anniversary.

After eating and watching movies, Bad Boy and the gem of Sapphire began to play video games and get to know each other better. Sapphire lost a game to Bad Boy that she was usually good at, all because she kept looking at his chocolate lips, imagining what they could one day possibly do to her. She did this to the point of distraction, then annoying frustration, which led her to say out of nowhere, "I'm curious!" in the middle of the game. Her thoughts got the best of her.

This left Bad Boy in total confusion, thinking she was talking about the game they were playing. Still holding his joystick, he looked at her, puzzled. "What happened?!"

She was looking at his lips and getting up at the same time, repeating, "I'm curious." She sat down on his lap, facing him and kissing him. "Your lips drive me crazy!"

"What I do?!" Bad Boy asked.

"Nothing! That's what makes me even more curious!"

She started kissing him more while secretly unbuttoning his shirt. Then as she was peeling it off, it all finally computed in his head what she was curious about.

"Girl, you better quit playing before we end up cracking the seal on that thing!"

He kissed her back, saying her little fingers were working quick as magic, because before he knew, it she had her hands on his situation, stroking him to the point where precum started coming out.

"Whoa!" He gently grabbed her hand and said, "Where did all that come from, Ma?"

"Just looking at you rattles my chain and makes me want to do what I ain't done!" By this, she meant that she had never had sex. She grabbed his jawn again, then left, leading him into a state of total confusion.

Grabbing her hand again, Marty gently said to her, "Let's talk about this..."

"That we already did! It's time to up the ante in this game we playin'! I need to know what this feeling that seemed to set me on fire is. Just hearing your voice... looking at them lips... Talk to me," Sapphire said.

"WHAT THEY SAY, YO?!" He was laughing and moving her hand off his situation that was beefin' harder than Chinese arithmetic!

"Stop playing! I wanna know 'bout that good joog that

have the ladies all up in their feelings, ready to steal, kill and destroy like the devil!" Sapphire said.

"You keep holding onto my man down there, you really gonna find out!" he said, moving her hand again.

"We got all night to do this, but the name of the game ain't gon' be 'You Keep Moving My Hand Off Your Man.' That's what it ain't gon' be! "

"What's it gonna be called, then? 'Cause I'm trying to be a gentleman," Bad Boy said.

"It's gonna be called 'Let's Get It'! Another game you can save for them chickens who already know, but playing like they don't! Let's get it!" Sapphire said.

"Let's get it, then…" Bad Boy said.

She put her mouth on him, remembering how her cousin demonstrated how to make a man happy when they bought bullets from the ice cream truck.

He pulled that thing out her mouthpiece, even though she had a pistol grip on it! Then, he went down on her like he wanted to devour her! When she couldn't take it anymore, she grabbed that thing and slightly pressed it against herself, moving it up and down until she could ease right on top of it.

From there, she began breaking gears down like you would a 18-wheeler until they both fell asleep with her on top of him.

When he woke back up, he felt himself still up in her tail. His man started throbbing, and off to the races they went.

Feeling like she was a horse jockey, she grabbed the hat hooked on the headboard—an Arizona Cardinals fitted cap. She put it on backwards, then leaned forward into what became the finish line.

"Now I know what the business is and why them gals be going cuckoo for cocoa puffs!"

"Do ya?!" Bad Boy asked as he pulled off the Magnum wearing and threw it in the garbage can. She had never seen him put it on.

"Good game, coach!" she said when she realized what he had done. They both started laughing. He had to pee, so he headed to the restroom, peed and then turned on the jacuzzi. He poured some of that Gucci body wash in it to bubble that thing up for the next go-round.

Feeling good that he had broken a thoroughbred, he was definitely in high spirits again and secretly on Ese's level, which was many steps in front of him.

If only Bad Boy knew…

Waking up the next day, everybody came out of their hotel rooms well-slept and well-kept. So, they decided to go on down to breakfast at Cabo's restaurant.

Looking at Bad Boy, Ese knew what went down. He knew how Bad Boy's steelo always changed gears, breaking him down to some happiness.

Bad Boy was also doing his own investigation and found that Ese had piped down a lot and been joyful, smiling all the time. It made him a better person.

Walah and Jennifer had peeped game from the gate, as they saw reflections of themselves in true love going out to pasture. On many levels, these men would all be changed for the better.

In life, nothing is promised to you, not even tomorrow. God alone holds that key, leaving no one to know the day, hour or year of His return. We just have to stay ready, not get ready, in preparation for the coming of your very King.

Lil Mama had fallen right back into the groove of things at the store. She also knew that the fashions she had been holding onto weren't hitting the numbers that they used to, so she knew it was time to regroup on a new level.

Her daughters would soon be 13. They were quite fashionable and creative, since their Great Grands had taught them how to sew. They had mastered making their clothes; it was an art for them. Just seeing different items on other people and adding a touch of their own, they came up with a clothing line of their own called "A Touch of Class," using a lot of the vintage clothing designs that Great Grands and her twin sister used to sew. They mixed and matched the patterns, bringing them into a fashion of their own and leaving other girls their age or older inquiring about their outfits.

Periodically, the girls often placed a few of their outfits on display. When they did, it would cause a stir that led crowds into the store.

After running a couple of trial runs, Lil Mama's daughters were inspired to discuss the business aspects of things. This motivated them to excel in their schoolwork in order to find more time to create different designs. Eventually, they brought their hopes and dreams to the dinner table in front of their parents, who were very proud of their two girls. Their daughters had learned and mastered things they never heard of— cooking, baking and sewing, which all led them and inspired them to become young entrepreneurs who always succeeded in all their money-making endeavors.

After making their parents' favorite dish of beef enchiladas, refried beans and tacos, Big Big led Lil Lil into the desire to market their clothing line. This got their parents' attention.

"What would you call this clothing line?" Lil Mama asked.

"A Touch of Class, in bold red letters," Lil Lil said.

"What will the line consist of? Tyrik asked.

"Shirts, pants, blouses, swimwear, dresses and wedding dresses," Big Big replied.

Lil Lil excused herself and came back with a clothing

rack on wheels that had a variety of things they spoke of in different colors, sizes and samples.

Seeing them, their parents knew that they were serious about what they wanted. Tyrik and Lil Mama both also knew that, like the girls' grandma, Luscious Bell, once they made their minds up, there would be no changing them back.

"On the business aspect, we would have to get your line registered, as well as the lines of those who would eventually make the bulk of your merchandise," their mom said.

"That's just it. We would like to keep it personal, online, made-to-order," Big Big said.

"Then, if it's set off into the big leagues, we'll go from there," Lil Lil added.

"Colors? Materials?" Lil Mama asked.

"We did the research, and there are factories in Philadelphia where Great Grands lives," Big Big said.

Knowing all of that, this was just a formality to get their parents' blessing, 'cause they already knew Granny Warbucks would back their project and have hands-on, day-to-day oversight. Win, lose or draw, Great Grands didn't care. These two girls were living out the dream she and her sister had wished for when they were younger, but didn't have the money it took for start off.

As they grew into their own their plans, life took its own direction with the men they loved, who were also twins.

"I'm okay with it if your mother is. She makes the rules," Tyrik said.

"No, *we* make the rules, husband," Lil Mama said. "I'm good with it. Now, my surprise to you all is... I'm three months pregnant!"

"Yay!" they all cheered.

"With triplets!"

"Triplets!" the twins gasped.

"Boys! Lil Mama added.

Upon hearing this news, Tyrik was up, happily dancing around. He hit bullseye times three this round!

"That's what I'm talking about!" he exclaimed.

"Wait 'til you up at night with them boys!" Lil Mama laughed. "With that out of the way, the next thing I want to talk about is the trip I need to take. You ladies and gentlemen are welcome to accompany me."

"I would, but I got to hold down the fort," Tyrik replied.

"That leaves us ladies!"

"While we're there, we can check out our business venture," Big Big said.

"Call Great Grands and ask her if she wants to go when Ese and Bad Boy come back."

One girl started dialing and the other started cleaning the table while their mom looked like she wanted to help, but was too full to do so.

"It's all good, Mom," Lil Lil said.

"Sure is, but we're not cutting you no slack for your little basketball-head boys," Big Big said.

"Watch your mouth, little Big!" Lil Mama laughed.

"Great Grands must be at the casino cashing in them tokens she be coming up on."

"Oh, yeah! I forgot that's where she said she was going!" Lil Mama said. "So, girls, how y'all feel about having brothers for real?"

"It's going to be fun to see three of Daddy running around here, chasing after himself times three!" Lil Lil replied.

"How do you know they gon' look like they daddy and not like you?!" Big Big pressed.

"Ain't that the truth, baby!" their mother said, laughing.

"What y'all laughing at, Charlie's devils?!" Tyrik asked.

"They talking 'bout it's gonna be three mini yous chasing you around in saggy diapers, trying to get the gangsta lean on! Yaaa Meannn!" Big Big said jokingly.

"Gone on wit' dat!" Tyrik said. After thinking about it, he too had a laugh, since it was said like that! No one had any complaints as they all headed to the family room.

They turned the TV on to the *T.I. and Tiny* TV show they watched faithfully as a family, then *Love and Hip Hop* that followed. But that all changed as Great Grands came in hollering.

"I won $10,000!"

"That's good, 'cause we got something you can invest it in," Lil Lil said.

"I got you! I got you, baby girl. Ain't that how they say it in the streets?" Great Grands said. That had the whole family rolling.

Big Big got up and said, "I got Mama bathroom."

"Well, I guess that means I got the hall bathroom," the other twin chimed in.

Usually after watching TV, it was time for the girls to take a bath. They usually alternated bathrooms, since their mother's bathroom was the best.

"I'm just playing, sis. You right. We take turns, 'cause I know you like the bubbles." She knew her sister would be upset if she used their mother's bathroom, but she wouldn't say anything to keep the peace.

The next week went by in lightning speed, then it was time for the spring fling at Penn State College.

The fellas had already bought the fits they would need, so as time was winding up, they used it doing other things besides shopping, if you know what I mean.

The rappers that were performing were Trina the

Baddest, Trick Daddy and 50 Cent.

It went all the way down in a real way. Everyone had a good time, but a couple dudes got their wigs split by coming at "The Baddest" incorrectly!

From there, the group went out to eat at Del Frisco's and got full as a tick, then headed back to the telly to spend quality time with each other.

The good thing was that they all agreed on was to use no telephones other than room service. This was the best decision for all, as they wanted their time together.

Jennifer, Sapphire and Jasmine had all become close friends and had begun to hang out.

They spent their last day on the east coast riding a boat, kayaking and water skiing. They ate on the restaurant boat that sailed through Penn's Landing, which made that day even more fun and memorable.

Upon making it back to their hotel, they were full. Jennifer and the other girls all headed to the beauty spa, while the fellas watched the game on TV.

By the time they got back, the game was over and the fellas were back in their rooms, waiting for the return of their ladies and 100 percent one-on-one time. The rest of the night would be theirs, and they would hold these moments until the girls graduated from school.

Bad Boy started his off with a body massage.

Ese started and finished his off with lovemaking, trying to make sure he didn't shoot no blanks!

Jennifer and Walah had talks till late into the night, and made love passionately till the early morning sunshine burst in.

Saying goodbye was a tearful event—not just for the ladies, but for the fellas as well. No matter how tough we men act, we get it in when it comes to the breezies. Keep it 100!

Bad Boy, Ese and Walah had the driver drop each lady off at their desired places; from there, they were off to the airport to head westbound. Excitedly, they talked about their trip and about the spring fling. This was supposed to be their main purpose, but they all were scared to really look at the money shots. If reckless eyeballing was really a crime, they would all be in prison, because they ended up seeing a lot more than they all thought. They exposed themselves as they played the "Did you see this? Did you see that?" game, only to find that all of them had seen the green AND in between… not to mention getting they gangsta lean!

Making it all back to Arizona soil, touching down and immediately going off to running their business was the plan for   Ese and Bad Boy. They had to make up for what they spent, which—for real, for real—was all out of M&M's pockets.

First things first, they would go to M&M's house to get

their game tight and the items they purchased.

Right when they walked in, M&M was sitting by the TV, watching a movie. He turned it off when he saw them. "Why didn't you tell me you were going to Philly, son? " So many things were going through Bad Boy's godfather's mind, as he was in the place that his mother had gotten killed. M&M had never wanted to go back there.

"I needed to see if I could handle it. How did it work out?"

"Good. When I read your text, then received the boxes, I knew…" his godfather said.

"Did you put the Goodfellas on me?" Bad Boy asked.

"I should have, when I realized you were being sneaky," M&M laughed. "I'm glad all went well. How did it go for you, nephew?"

"Good…" Ese said meekly.

"I would agree, seeing that nice ring on your finger."

Bad Boy had somehow missed it, and almost broke his neck looking at Ese's finger.

Ese changed the subject quickly. "Tio, did you see what I got you?"

"I would have, if I had opened the box."

"I put your name on your box. Why wouldn't you open it, Tio?"

"Let me see..." M&M checked the box. "It sure does have my name on it."

He opened the box, and at the bottom, there was a sexy two-piece swimsuit. "Who's this for?!"

"For your lady across the street."

M&M laughed so hard that he cried alligator tears. When he was able to talk and breathe after all the laughter, he said, "Imagine that!"

"Can't do it! She's all you, Tio!" Ese said.

"You paid $200 for this?!" M&M asked.

"That's how my godfather gets down!"

"She'll get the gift. Don't worry, fellas."

"Have her model them for you. Let her know you still got skill," Ese said.

"I will... I will," M&M said.

"Now, down to business, Pops," Bad Boy said. "Double what we usually hit for."

"Yes, Massa!" M&M said jokingly.

From there, they all went to work. M&M had been getting bored. Even though he had spent a week with his grandkids while his son was away, plus across the street a few times, he never got tired of popping clips or clocking chips—he always said he wouldn't stop till his heart popped!

As he got older, his fan club began to disappear 'cause

he wasn't making it rain in every direction like he used to.

Bad Boy found it truly humbling, as he felt that he really had no friends, but it was okay. He could truly say he saved himself a lot of heartaches and headaches. At the end of the day, all we really have is God and our families.

Bad Boy finished his drops and headed to work at the gym. He was happy to be going to work at a place where he was at peace.

Lately, he had been having dreams about trying to save his mother, only to find that he needed to save himself from being shot. He just didn't understand it; the more he tried, the more confused he became.

Sometimes, he wondered if it was guilt that he was experiencing because his mother lost her life trying to save his. Other times, he thought it was some type of sign or subliminal message.

The vacation he took was a much-needed getaway. He was able to talk to Sapphire about his STDs that he had transmitted to the baby that could possibly be his.

Looking back at the night that the girl had told him it was his baby, he thought about the dream he had been having prior to the incident—how real the gunshot wound to his chest felt. The fight that he had with his mother about the gun, as the bullet took her life.

His godfather said, "Boo, boo, boo."

CPSIA information can be obtained
at www.ICGtesting.com
Printed in the USA
BVHW010838150322
631519BV00002B/86